THE ABERRATION

Kevin Sheehan

THE ABERRATION

Library of Congress Control Number 2012944904

ISBN 978-0-945980-53-7

Cover design by Jeanne H. Lachance

FOR HEATHER

Chapter 1

LOONWATER

Sebago Lake crested three feet above the high water mark in Raymond, Maine, on June 20, 1959, persistent spring rains having swelled Portland's reservoir faster than the city and the S. D. Warren paper company in Westbrook could draw it down. Loonwater, the ten acres I had inherited from my mother, Henrietta "Nettie" Pineo, looked like an island for once instead of part of the north shore of Jordan Bay. This year the boulder breakwater connecting it to Burnside Island was submerged, and the channel separating it from the mainland wasn't choked with eel grass and pine stumps. I no longer had to apologize for it.

At least not to Witte Murch, twenty-one and barely four hours my wife, who stood hugging herself at the west window of Pooh's Cabin. For a moment she remained still, her close-set gray eyes reflecting the ripples on Turtle Pond inlet while the late afternoon light from the lake played across her slender smile. Then she sighed and turned to address me. "It's just like you said, dear."

Between us in the center of the worn pine floor lay our duffel and provisions for a week. I had been pacing between the bed and the door, scrutinizing the musty cedar half-log camp I'd bunked in for seventeen of my twenty-one summers, noting the dusty dozen army blankets draped over the collar ties that had gone four years without shaking, the cobweb-festooned fieldstone fireplace and the cone of sawdust on the door sill left by carpenter ants still audibly gnawing at the lintel.

"No, it's not," I said, suppressing the undiminished thrill at hearing her call me "Dee-ah" for the umpteenth time. "Mom would be horrified. Just look at this." I shoved open the screen door and kicked at the sawdust cone, scattering the resinous powder across the rotting porch planks like so much dance floor wax. The door spring sprinkled me with rust, twanged at full extension and reluctantly returned the feeble frame. I caught the door and flung it wide, stepped outside and, defying Nettie's decree, allowed it to slam behind me.

The bang was much louder than I expected, and it started the tape loop going inside my head; so, instead of the familiar wooden clap, my brain conjured the crack of Nettie's twenty-two. I had shrunk to a boy of seven, marooned on her insular sanctum for the summer, a small penitent pawn crushed by guilt.

When the crumbling door screen predictably shattered from the impact and dusted me once more with rust, Nettie was there, towering over me, fuming. Her sarcasm was as sharp on my wedding day as the knife she'd plunged into her heart to end her life on December 15, 1956: "Karcher, if you're trying to get my attention, you have it."

I shook my head, trying to banish Nettie's ghost, descended the moss-covered steps and circled the cabin. Decay and neglect were everywhere: the toppled gray birch leaning against the north gable, roots exposed, bracket fungus blooming from its trunk; the steaming thatch of pine spills piled inches deep on the roof; the scattered stack of kindling under the porch. I bent to pick up the stump of a deer leg lying next to the sticks. As the blood rushed to my head, my brain reverted to reality.

"The damn hunters took all the hardwood and left this," I called, thumping the rigid appendage against the cabin and holding it up to the window. "And all the screens have rusted to smithereens. I just can't keep up."

Softly, through the open window, came a reedy refrain, like the windblown wail of a distant cord wood saw at sunset:

> This ole house is a-gettin' shaky;
> This ole house is a-gettin' old.
> This ole house lets in the rain;
> This ole house lets in the cold.
> Ain't got time to fix the shingles;
> Ain't got time to fix the floor.
> Ain't got time to oil the hinges
> Nor to mend no window panes.

"It's not funny, Witte," I snapped, reentering the cabin. "This is a damn disaster, and here you are, lolling on the bed, joking. Your dad sure named you right, only he couldn't spell."

"Watch it, Buster."

Witte's regional bark—Bus-tah—was unmistakable, but in my vulnerable state, her loud reprimand at close range triggered a vision of Nettie's ruddy, full moon face inches from mine, her hand raised and closing fast. Instinctively, I braced for the blow.

Nothing happened.

Cautiously, I looked up. Between the pointed pine bedposts I saw the long face of mock compassion, complete with pity pout and steeply raked eyebrows flanking deep forehead furrows that shaded eyes the size of flywheels.

"That how you treat a bride?"

"Uh, n...no. No, m'am. Sorry."

"You better be."

I was about to apologize again, but Witte had turned her attention to more pressing matters. She was squirming about on the mattress, testing the loft of the flaccid kapok. Twice she stopped to strike a distracting pose, presumably for my benefit. "This rack's lot better than my cot at the Beach."

She swung her legs over the rail and sat up. "We forgot somethin', dear. You're supposed to carry me over the threshold."

"We'll fix that," I said, scooping her up and bearing her to the door. "But first, you need cooling off." I started for the lake.

"Oh, no, you don't," was quickly followed by a burst of rib tickling that forced me to lose my grasp. Freed, Witte dashed for the cabin and sprawled on the steps to block my return. As I approached, she lowered her head, allowing her smoky tresses to fall over her face, so that all I could see was the cutting edge of her long winter nose. Then she tossed her head to clear her vision and scowled. "Now, look, I'm doin' this *once—now—*with *you.*"

Witte's cast iron resolve rivaled Nettie's, and never failed to raise a tear. I missed my one-eighth Cree mother most of all here, at Loonwater, where for two months each year she drank no hard liquor and produced meals without fail, where her love of the outdoors beat back her insanity, where I learned from her how to swim, whittle, tend a fire, handle small boats, prime a pump and use an ax. Could Witte fill Nettie's moccasins? And if she did, would she, too, go berserk and kill herself in a flash of fury?

No, this woman was different. Witte's signals were steady as Portland Head Light. The contrast in stability between the two women in my life was as strong as their presence in it. And yet, here on Nettie's island mausoleum, I had trouble discriminating one from the other. It had to do with dominance; both women had taken command of my soul.

I advanced instinctively under orders from northern eyes of gray. Witte rose to meet me with an intensity of purpose that would have made General Patton blush. Jaw set, she wound her arms about my neck, draped herself across my outstretched arms and whispered in my ear, "Chores can wait till morning, dear."

Was this really me holding for keeps a woman so warm and fatally scented, so finely carved and plushly upholstered, so single-minded and secure? I wanted to pinch myself, but I didn't have a hand free.

A split second later, as if Witte had read my mind, I got the jolt I needed. My distraction had stalled the procedure sufficiently to require a prod in the pelvis from a long oval fingernail. Alerted, I hooked a corner of what was left of the screen door with my toe and made passage for us. I'd barely framed the opening when Witte planted a sopping smooch that obliterated my view and caused me to trip on the sill. Staggering to regain my balance, I managed to juggle her to the foot of the bed where I let her fall in a heap of hysterics.

"That wasn't very smooth, Karcher," she spluttered between spasms, pulling me down on top of her. There was something symbiotic about the way our bodies contacted, like flint and steel, requiring very little relative motion to generate a spark.

"God, you're lofty," I groaned. "Let's skip supper and just make love."

Witte looked at her watch. Barely able to draw a breath with my weight on her chest, she croaked, "It's nearly six, Karcher. I'm hungry. And you must be starved. We don't want to get started and poop out."

It was beginning to sound like an endurance test, but I knew from experience that Witte was speaking strictly from her gut and had no performance standard in mind, so I suggested we open a can of Snow's oyster stew.

Witte looked over her imaginary half frames. "I'll make a spinach salad with lots of mushrooms. Did we get bacon? Can't make spinach salad without bacon."

By this time we were on the floor on our hands and knees, rummaging through the box of goodies we'd picked up at Maines's Store in South Casco and two farms along Raymond Cape Road on our way in. The bacon was there — Jordan's hickory smoked, of course. The spinach from Horace Libby looked a bit wilted but salvageable. Ruby Winslow had taken to Witte and wouldn't let her pay for the eggs. "Call it a weddin' present," she'd said. "Karcher got a good one when he caught you."

"Let's see this kitchen of yours," Witte demanded, lofting our twenty-five pound box of provisions with alarming ease and making for the door. I grabbed the kerosene and water cans and followed suit, calling ahead, "We'll get the ice tomorrow. Stuff'll keep okay in the small chest tonight."

Witte led the procession from Pooh's to the main cabin, Friends and Relations, balancing the carton on her head. I kept my distance to enjoy a full frame of her stately progress, marveling at the stillness of her shoulders, the sway of her hips, and the lilt of her feet falling surely in the winding carpet of pine spills. Half way, at the twin pines that still supported my childhood swing, she paused. "Look, dear. The lady slippers are still in bloom. Aren't they precious?"

"Lovely," I replied, unable to take my eyes off her.

* * * * * *

The afternoon breeze off the lake had lost its strength to turn the aspen leaves and stir the sibilant pines. With the hush came a nip in the air, reminding me to bring in wood and start the fire. Groceries sorted and stashed, I headed for the log shelter. Fortunately, the hunters had left our supply of two-footers intact, and the kindling box beside the fireplace was still full of pine snaps.

Four armloads of splits filled the main wood box. My trips to and from the lean-to, punctuated by numerous slams of the screen door and thunderous rumblings from the resonant spruce box accepting its charge, elicited a raised eyebrow and a pointed remark from Witte already at home in the tiny kitchen. "Moose in this house'd be quiet as a mouse compared to you."

I broke up the kindling under a pillow and laid the fire a twig at a time, tiptoeing across the hearth like the mouse Witte preferred to the moose. Using birch bark as tinder, I fashioned a fuse from the longest strip and lit the end. When the main wad of bark began to sputter and send its smoky orange flame to lick the inside of the firebox, Witte appeared in the wings.

"Sorry, dear. I got awful rattled. Hunger does that to me." She stood for a moment, watching the sparks burst from the kindling and the curved sheet of flame build against the firebrick. "Fire smells good."

Witte had lost her composure. I could tell from the restlessness of her gaze and the way she nibbled on her prominent lower lip that more than hunger was responsible for her distress. It wasn't like her to guard her feelings too closely.

"Penny for your thoughts?"

Witte drew a deep sigh. "I'm worried about cha, Karcher. Something about this place don't set right with you."

"How's supper coming?"

Witte's eyes hardened and moved from the fire to me. "Don't deny it. You've been some ugly since we landed."

"Like you, I can't think well on an empty stomach," I dodged again, looking away to avoid her penetrating stare, knowing full well it wouldn't work.

Witte swung a leg over the hearth bench and pulled up square in front of me. Her lips were tightly drawn, and she was breathing forcefully through her nose. "There'll be no supper till we get this settled. Now, what's eating you?"

The blood rushed to my face, and I began to shake. Wisely, Witte loosened my noose. Moving closer, she spilled her sable silk in my lap, curled over and looked up, wearing a wicked smirk. "You didn't need fuel fifteen, ten minutes ago."

"Okay, okay. You've got me eating nothing out of your hand. I'll give you a five-minute summary, then I'm going to lock you in the kitchen.

"I keep seeing my mother in your form here—her ghost; it's disturbing the hell out of me. When you speak, it's her talking, and I obey her—you—like a little kid. God, I hate to think of you that way.

"You're not at all like her. She was stocky, mannish and dishonest. But she gave direct orders, like you. Trouble was, she marched to the beat of a delirious drummer. Your timekeeper is steady as a metronome."

"Am I that predictable, dear?"

"It's not so much repetition, as dependability. You're exciting without being eccentric."

"Think you can tolerate some sanity?"

I winced at the instant incision. Witte had outclassed Nettie's best offense, and yet somehow I neither feared nor despised her for the attack. Had my mother displayed such insight, I might have benefited. As it happened, her caustic scolding was seldom timely or accurate, and so I mistrusted her motives, however well intended. Alcohol has a way of potentiating neurosis.

With one bold stroke, Witte had hacked her way to the heart of my dilemma. Psychological chaos had been so pervasive during my formative years that I had actually grown accustomed to it. I shunned normal behavior. Sane people, the kind I found outside my home, seemed lifeless and trivial, not worth knowing. In my confusion, I felt special being born into insanity.

"I asked you a question, Karcher."

"Sorry. You nicked a vein, and I'm dazed from the blood loss.

"I confess I somehow miss the madness. Even here there was never a secure moment. I had to be constantly on guard because Nettie's mind games never flagged. If I relaxed a minute, she would classify me with Dad as 'worse than useless.' God forbid I should make a rational suggestion; she'd shake her head in disgust and mutter, *'Non compos mentis.'*

"But with you there's no game. You're sincere. I don't know how to cope with that."

Witte propped herself up on one elbow, pulled a shallow breath, brushed her hair aside and took aim. "I'm just tryin' to get you to see how long the train is you're pullin'. You gotta shunt some freight or you're never going to make the grade. It's too heavy, Karcher." She forced the final sentence from her throat with the last vestige of air left in her lungs. My name emerged as little more than a croak.

Witte never risked losing a point by pausing to breathe mid- thought. She budgeted her air; when it was gone, her discourse was done. It made for economy of words.

I treasured her guttural finales almost as much as I did her down East delivery, but this time my discomfort with the subject overshadowed my enjoyment.

Before I could react to her metaphor, she had popped to her feet. "Now, I need the buckets filled. And the stove'll need fuel before breakfast." Without waiting for my answer, she deliberately ground off the ten paces to the kitchen, padding the pine with her dainty bare feet. She knew I'd be watching.

As firelight replaced the twilight, the cabin shrank in the cedar-orange glow. I lit one of the three Aladdin mantle lamps and turned the wick low, as Nettie had taught me, to prevent blackening the chimney when the burner warmed up. In the kitchen, I stopped to light the sconce over the stove, and accidentally bumped Witte's right breast in the process. She was reaching for a tin of strike-anywhere Ohio Blue Tips on the shelf when my elbow found its mark. Before I could bend down to drag the two overturned pails from under the sink, she enveloped me in sultry shadow, breathing between nibbles on my left earlobe, "Any more of that and there'll be no supper at all."

"Sorry, I..."

"No excuses." One little hand covered my mouth while another gave me a pat on the behind and headed me out the door, pails in tow, for the dock.

When I reached the water's edge, I set the pails in the sand, filled my lungs with the still, cool air laden with birch smoke and watched the full moon rise, a huge, tallow balloon in the mist. Bass were surfacing for mayflies in the cove, initiating rings that grew until they intersected on the surface. A loon called for his mate out beyond Burnside Island, but there was no answer. It was a lonely sound, one that the abandoned only child within me could understand.

"K-a-r-c-h-e-r," came a clarion call from the cabin.

Instinctively, I took up the pails and moved silently along the dock to its end. Nettie was right behind me, coaching. "A Native American never disturbs the water more than he has to." I floated the pails on the surface, gently listing each until it filled to the crimp line and swung plumb.

"K-A-R-C-H-E-R," louder, from the porch.

"C-o-m-i-n-g," I called back, indignant for having to break the stillness of a Sebago summer evening. The bails creaked and clanked as I yanked the pails from the lake and stumped the planks, slopping water with each frustrated footfall. Was my new taskmaster to be more demanding than the last?

Witte held open the screen door as I entered. "Thought you'd drowned or gone fishin'. Supper's near ready."

"I'll prime the pump in the morning," I replied, searching for a sliver of autonomy, but it wasn't enough. I was angry for allowing Witte to terminate Nettie's ritual.

"We have a tradition around here of doing chores slowly and silently," I sputtered, eyeballing Witte narrowly, "...so as not to miss a moment of nature's choreography. Sometimes that means stopping to sniff, pausing to peruse, taking time to touch that which lies in our path. Loonwater has been left intentionally primitive to foster relaxed communication with the outdoors. 'Easy does it,' as Nettie would say."

Witte smiled smugly. "Thought I heard Nettie pounding her fist up there when the wood box was being filled."

The pain of recognizing my double standard only served to further fuel our feud. Supper was spent in silent stalemate under Aladdin's mantle, the two of us glaring at each other across the peeled pine trestle table.

From the anthracitic sheen of her eyes, I quickly deduced that Witte would take no orders from Nettie. Tradition had no tenure for my practical pal. She was wiping the slate clean. Nettie was gone; she no longer ruled Loonwater or Karcher.

And neither did Witte. This was no takeover on her part, but an affirmation of independence. It was not a question of ownership. Loonwater and Karcher were there to be shared, shaped and enjoyed.

For me, the incurable romantic, the past held life's true treasure. I swam in a shore-less sea of mourning, groping for the fringe of gold atop each sunlit ripple that forever slipped, mere quicksilver, through my outstretched fingers.

It was a wonder we ever got along, given this sharp contrast in philosophy. Body chemistry alone, magnetic as it was, couldn't account for the match.

Our bond was stuck with more ethereal stuff. Each of us held a piece to life's puzzle that the other needed. Witte weighted the seesaw with reality, and I buoyed her end of the plank with fantasy. Together, we leveled the thing.

* * * * * * * *

Witte's fare was a feast fit for Epicurus, a culinary triumph in such unfamiliar and primitive quarters. She had come to terms with the kerosene and mouse tracks without so much as a whimper, more than I can say for Nettie who, after so many summers, should have been able to open camp without cursing.

"You're amazing," I said, breaking the deadlock. "I mean...this food...from that kitchen. Sorry to mess up your timing." I pulled an oil-stained white handkerchief from the back pocket of my jeans and waved it slowly between us. "Truce?"

Witte dropped her gaze, put down her fork, leaned back in Nettie's chair and tried hard not to smile. "Darn you. You're too cunnin' to stay mad at." Then, noting my half-empty plate, she found the excuse to frown. "Eat up all good, now. Dishwater's rollin'."

The Perfection stove reservoir took several gulps of air, and the battered tin wash kettle began to rattle in earnest. I leapt to my feet to lower the wick. Nettie would have set the flame for a boil coincident with the emptying of our plates, to conserve kerosene. How could Witte be expected to master the stove in one handshake?

"I cut her back a bit," I said, trying not to reveal my anxiety as I reseated myself, but the impatient kettle was still audible, so I wolfed down the last of Witte's supper and dashed for the stove, precariously busing our dishes to the sink on the way. Before Witte could respond to the clatter and my muffled cursing, I had doused the flame, scraped the scraps into the wet garbage box, burned myself mixing the wash water in the green oval basin on the right and guessed at the rinse water temperature I'd just finished tempering in the matching white basin on the left before a nostalgic whiff of vaporized kerosene from the still-hot stove wick choked me to a stop. There I stood, frozen mid-frenzy, sniffling over the sink, unable to believe Nettie was gone.

Witte kept her distance when she came in, took up a dish towel and waited for me to recover. Slowly, I picked up rhythm and began washing the glasses. By the time I got to the plates, I could focus well enough to crush an ant ambling along the sliding barn sash sill. The lightning movement of my soapy right fist momentarily interrupting the flow of dishes from right to left, raised a chuckle from my partner. I turned toward the unfamiliar sound.

"He won't have the guts to do that again," I said as I disposed of the disemboweled insect, trying to buoy Witte's levity and banish Nettie from the room.

Under the lamp's glow I saw Witte's cautious smile, a tenuous flicker that faded to a long question mark with two glistening, slightly separated incisors forming the dot. Witte felt her presence too. Nettie was still in her kitchen.

In unison, we spoke, "I gotta get out of here." We laughed uncomfortably at the coincidence, knowing it was no coincidence.

"It'll be better tomorrow, in the daylight," I offered, not at all sure of what I was saying.

"I feel creepy, dear, like there's someone else here. After we finish, I wanna go for a row."

"Good idea. I need some air."

It was a shaky little hand that dropped the last fork in the drawer and retracted the wick in the sconce. Witte had barely the breath to huff out the flame. I'd not seen her like that since the night before Christmas, 1956, when, less than two weeks after Nettie's suicide, Nettie's lesbian lover, Bente, had tried to forcibly seduce her.

I screened the fire and got us wraps, grabbed a flashlight, and guided my trembling bride out into the moonlight. We shambled to the lake, arm in arm, one unsteady shadow among the still pines. At the end of the dock we stood, listening. Only the solo of a sanguinary mosquito, the banjo glug of a green frog and the squeak of a little brown bat disturbed the silence. Over the water, the air, still drawing heat from the lake, was almost balmy. I felt the change and peeled off my Filson windbreaker, but Witte continued to shiver under the Hudson's Bay Point blanket I'd wrapped around her. Below us, half shrouded in mist, was Nettie's pine-green Rangely, dew glistening on its gunwales and foredeck.

"Why don't you pull for a while to get warm," I suggested, wiping the moisture from the thwarts with my truce flag. "I'11 spell you when you're up to temperature."

Without answering, Witte crouched aboard, clutching her outsized woolen shawl. I set the locks and shipped the oars for her before casting off and settling in the stern sheets. "You'll feel much better by the time we reach Burnside's. I promise."

For most of a minute we drifted. Then, as I watched, exquisite little hands appeared from under the blanket and reached out for the grips. The shawl fell away, revealing an incomparable, seated silhouette whose torso bulged below the shoulders and fairly disappeared at the waist, filling out again at the hips to a substantial base which took command of better than half of the narrow bow thwart. A spasm surged through my groin, and before I could stop myself, I said, "God, you're gorgeous, even in two dimensions and the black and white of night."

The oars, which had just been positioned for the first stroke, were peremptorily withdrawn with a roar through the locks. "Now, look. How am I supposed to set a course with a moonstruck coxswain?"

Witte leaned forward and rested her elbows on the crossed looms to await my response. Even though she was backlighted, I could detect the restrained mirth in her eyes, and knew she was coming around. I pointed over her right shoulder in the direction of the tiny island that terminated the breakwater. "Port engine full ahead; starboard engine ahead, slow."

"Aye, aye, Captain." Witte snapped a salute and fell to the oars, pulling hard with her right until my finger took dead aim for her nose, whereupon she synchronized throttles and held her course.

The sodden old Rangely carried marvelously between urges from the ash breeze, thanks to its inertia and fine lines, allowing Witte to set a relaxed rocking rhythm, which only served to further fan my flames. Her protracted panting, which gradually became audible as she warmed under load, and the hull surging under me heightened the sensual illusion of coupling to the extent that I felt compelled to look away and force an image of her father's one-lunger pumping power to the Murch farm during the Thanksgiving 1955 blackout. The diversion was not entirely successful, as the aroma drifting aft from the "engine room" was not of warm iron and partly oxidized hydrocarbons, but the heady bouquet of Chanel Russia Leather and feminine exertion.

"Bearing, please, Sir."

"On course," I replied, jerking to attention. "Say, you must be plenty warm by now," I added quickly, attempting to suppress the compulsion to put the blocks to her right there, adrift and below decks. "I'll take her from here."

"Oh, will you, now?"

I blushed inconspicuously in the moonlight. The Rangely "engines" stalled, and we glided to within fifty yards of the lee shore of Burnside Island before losing way. Observing Witte continuing to pull deep breaths as the abating flush of propulsion was replaced by her building rush of desire, I abandoned my proper plan to spell her, and surrendered to the inevitable.

When I made no move for the helm, Witte shrugged and set about, stowing the oars, pulling the stretchers, sponging the bilge and spreading the blanket on the floor boards. When she was finished, she parked herself athwart-ships on the floor, her knees drawn to her chest, and patted the spot she had picked out for me. I reached for her hand, slid off the stern seat and took my place facing her.

The Rangely was a bony love nest, but more capacious and conforming than the flatiron skiff a coed and I had appropriated during my freshman fall at Field. After getting soaked and bruised trying to maneuver under that skiff's low thwarts, I wasn't keen on attempting to make love again in a small boat. But Witte's competent preparations were reassuring; there was a practiced balance to her shifting that expressed experience with nautical affairs. I had forgotten how obstreperous she could become when Aphrodite took possession of her senses.

"Better drop the hook," I advised, gauging our drift. "We don't want to ground out mid stroke."

Witte grinned wickedly, rolled over the thwarts and let go the Danforth, then crawled aft, sweeping the bilge with her dusky tresses, eyes fixed on her target, her body describing serpentine switchbacks in the moonlight. I felt the boat rock to the sway of her hips as the stern slowly settled to its former attitude. A moment later the moon was eclipsed, and I foundered in a sea of sweet saliva.

The Rangely listed hard to port as I fell back against the rail, trying to clear an air passage. I'd barely drawn a breath when the light went out of the night once more, and I found myself suffocating between moist mountains of overstuffed sweatshirt. The port gunwale shipped a chilly sheet of water, which ran down my neck, prompting a muffled expletive and a reflexive arching of my back, which only forced my face deeper into Witte's chest.

"Whoa, Witte-wench!" I gasped, having somehow managed to wrest free of her without capsizing our tiddly vessel.

"Captain take a Sebago shower?"

I tried to shift my weight toward the center of the boat, but found Witte had pinned me to port with her powerful thighs and child-bearing buttocks. "Doc won't have no trouble with me," she had confided during one of our prenuptial planning sessions under the boardwalk at Old Orchard Beach. "I'm not close-built, like some women."

Witte was losing control. Perspiration popped on her brow and upper lip, her breathing became labored and unsteady, and her hands trembled as they fumbled the buttons on my shirt. There wasn't much time left. If she spawned one of her spasms before I centered us, we'd surely wind up in the drink.

Secretly, I longed to experience another of her premature paroxysms. If I could just keep us afloat until her surface charge dissipated, our lovemaking could proceed at a safer, more stately pace. Besides, to quench her fire now with a burst of logic or enforced immersion seemed too cruel to contemplate; so, I scrunched lower in the bilge, edging us toward equilibrium.

Witte toyed with me like a lioness preparing to devour her prey. She was so busy panting, pawing and lapping me about the neck and face that she didn't detect the readjustment, even when my ears sank below the gunwale. As her lust built, she began to babble softly between slurps and nibbles. It was all I could do to keep my mind on the righting.

The Rangely had almost plumbed when Witte growled and tossed her head back, sending her hair aloft to fan the night like the Ferris wheel at Old Orchard Beach, slicing the moonlight to shards that sparkled among her silver highlights. I braced myself for the onslaught. This time I felt the tremor in her thighs locked astride my loins long before the throe descended, a tiny precursor to the quake. This time I had the pleasure of watching her torso take the impulse without restraint. This time I could treasure her ecstasy.

"No! Oh, my gosh! W...watch the boat. I'm...I'm goin'. Hold me, dear." Her head jerked to one side then the other. I reached up to support her shoulders as she arched her back, thrusting her bosom and listing the boat steeply to starboard. Fortunately, the Rangely parried the lurch and rolled upright without taking more water over the side. There was a rush of air from her throat, like the whoosh made by the Old Orchard Wurlitzer carousel organ dumping its vacuum for rewind. Then her shoulders slumped, her arms went rigid, and she drove her clenched fists into my solar plexus. The boat rocked fearfully but somehow managed not to capsize.

Witte bucked like an unbroken Arabian mare, clamped me in her most powerful vise and roared like the Cape Elizabeth diaphone. Her devastating thrusts would have certainly sent us overboard had they been executed at a higher elevation, but as they acted nearly dead on the Rangely's meta center, the boat just shuddered and sent out mini tidal waves.

A second later, she fell on me, spent and soaked. I held her until she recovered sufficiently to speak. The worst—and the best—was over. It was with some relief that I finally heard her ask: "Are we still afloat, dear?"

* * * * * * *

I failed Witte that first night at the lake. Instead of rising to her wondrous display of passion, I had listened to my recording of Nettie's counsel and become obsessed with Archimedes' self-righting moments, small craft safety and the absurdity of trying to make love in a round-bottomed rowboat.

My impotence persisted for the duration of the honeymoon. The old strip pine cradle never careened again, except once, when I clumsily stepped aboard to port with a full five-gallon can of kerosene. And ashore, only one bed sound screams in memory of our first sanctioned affair: the squeal of the peeled pine rail rolling in the bedpost sockets as we swung our legs over the side and slid to the floor each morning. It was a sound I had heard more than a thousand times during the seventeen summers I slept there. Sometimes, before falling asleep, I'd spin the rail just to hear it howl. It annoyed Nettie, but she never got around to fixing it, and it remained a relentless reminder of her.

After two weeks at the island, I was ready to call it quits, abandon Witte, go back to Connecticut and never return to Maine. What I really wanted to do was disappear from the face of the earth. It was not a death wish. Suicide could be painful and at the very least, ostentatious. Nettie had certainly demonstrated that. No, I wanted to vanish quietly, vaporize without ignition. But I stayed. Despite my humiliation, there was something about living with Witte, even platonically, that kept me at her side.

It must have been awful for her that first night, having to suddenly switch roles and become my nanny, but her transformation was as gracious as it was necessary. She spent the remainder of the night with me on the beach, trying in vain to stem my headlong plunge back in time.

In my brief reconstruction of unacceptable behavior, I had worked up a full-blown panic attack. All the familiar symptoms flourished: colic, chills, nausea, tingling and trembling extremities, lightheadedness, and an irresistible urge to keep moving.

We paced the sand for hours: I, blanket-wrapped, heaving deep breaths to hold down my supper; Witte alongside, coaxing while fanning me with a sheet of bark she'd peeled from a paper birch. The smaller I got, the less frightened I felt, so that by the time the moon set over Raymond Cape, I was once more a boy of seven under her arm, exhausted and sufficiently calm to sleep.

We left the Rangely on the sand and picked our way through the mist between the ghostly gray beeches lining the path to Pooh's. It was here, on the beach path among the granite boulders, where I first developed an identity. Here, before the two faces of Janus consumed Nettie, I was free to roam and find myself. Now, in the shadows of dawn, Mother Nature once more opened her womb for me, and I gratefully climbed inside to rest.

Chapter 2

WITTE'S WALTZ

The rotted pier pilings at Old Orchard Beach groaned under the press of a record July fourth crowd straining to hear Omar's gravelly gab. The savvy sage, looking precisely as I remembered him five years ago, in 1954, during Witte's and my first summer together, was fondling the palm of an effervescent blond. As he spoke, his blue eyes twinkled beneath a floppy black beret.

"You have a special talent," Omar was saying to the young woman as Witte and I came within earshot. He glanced at the man standing beside her, rolled a wizened cigar from one corner of his mouth to the other and chuckled. "No, it's not what your boyfriend, here, thinks. I'm talking about your avocation. You're very pretty, but good looks aren't paramount in your profession."

He worked her right middle finger between his sensitive thumb and forefinger, taking note of the callus on the inside of the first joint. "If I were your boss, I'd double your salary. A secretary that can take a hundred words a minute shorthand is a rare find.

"How did you know I was a secretary?" asked the blond. "And how could you tell I take shorthand that fast?"

Omar scribbled a few words on a small pad, put down his pencil and smiled. "My dear young lady, when you've been at this business as long as I have—almost sixty years—you learn to read the signs: a callus here, a free wrist there, a twitch of recognition in the eye when I get warm—it all leads me to you."

He bent toward the woman, still holding her gaze. "I'm seventy-eight years old. I've spent nearly a lifetime studying people. It's reached the point where I can usually place a person's profession within the first minute, just by reading their body language. Before I touch them."

The blond flinched imperceptibly, but Omar caught it. "Don't be frightened. I'm not a magician. I'm just a person, like you, with a career. My career is other people." He clasped her porcelain, manicured hand between his leathery palms. "Tell your boss you're worth every penny of the raise you're asking for. It's your turn to be rewarded." With that, he tore the sheet of paper from his pad and handed it to her. She blushed when she read what he had written: "A mirror reflects confidence, not beauty."

Neither Witte nor I were close enough to hear Omar's closing remarks to the woman, and the note was shared with no one, yet we both sensed, as we had the last time we met him, that he held a key to life's library of insight. Realizing the magnitude of the man, I suddenly felt sorry for him, having to grub a dollar from a passerby for a priceless nugget of his wisdom.

There was no resemblance whatever, yet Omar reminded me of my father, Professor Rackliff Owen Stickney, caught in the trap of life, guessing. It was also Dad's lot to impart guidance to the young: his anatomy students.

In his professorial garb, "Rack" was a pillar of competence, instilling a love for the grotesque, gelatinous organs and the interlocking, twisted tusks that hold us together. When I was fifteen, he showed me slides of a man's lip, black and distended with cancer, and of the excision and the contorted results following surgery, all designed to dissuade me from smoking a pipe, my only vice. I was disgusted. The pipe turned sour, I threw it in the garbage, my tongue healed, and I could taste again. He was right. But now he, too, was gone.

Dad's dilemma—whether to stay with Nettie or go it alone—was resolved by her suicide. But the divisive agony of trying to lead two lives—a Milquetoast ostrich at home, in New Sterling, Connecticut, ducking Nettie's psychoses; a monument in medical education at Stoughton University, in Manhattan—had been too much for his high tension heart. Dad died of a stroke a year and a half after Nettie took her life, in the city where he was born, Carlisle, England, on my twenty-first birthday. How could Dad have known that I would marry the woman he had proclaimed by far the best of those I'd brought to his doorstep, then botch the relationship in just a week? Could it be that I was meant to spend my adult life chaste in the company of antique one-cylinder stationary engines, those paragons of stability that had supplied order to my childhood of chaos?

With failure fresh on my mind, it seemed foolhardy to have forsaken iron for flesh. Women were for ogling, for touching perhaps, but never, never for trusting. They were, after all, only human, fallible like my departed father, and poor Omar, who, I reminded myself, had misjudged Witte as an airline stewardess in the summer of '54.

And yet, how could I mistrust this resolute woman whom my father had chosen, the one with engine-like consistency, unswerving devotion, exquisite proportions and enough passion to drive me to distraction? Why now, on our honeymoon, could I not let go and devour her, as I had that first summer here in the carousel's engine room while the organ blared, the gears gnashed, the children squealed and the colored lights played over our naked bodies?

Without realizing it, I had moved closer to Omar's booth, and then up to the window, and handed him my dollar for an answer to my dreadful dilemma. It was a desperate move, a public admission of failure. I was shaking and starting to shrink again. How could I phrase such a sensitive question?

"Remember us?" (Boy, was that dumb. How could he be expected to recognize us after five summers?) I began again. "You guessed my wife's occupation wrong five years ago, but gave her confidence to stick with me when I was tormented with self doubt. Well, I guess I'm still in the same boat, only now I'm married, and that's what worries me."

"Young man, relax. I'm not a marriage counselor, but I'd like to help, if I can. What is your name?"

"Karcher...Karcher Stickney."

"And this is your bride, this luscious lady here? Her name is?"

"Witte, sir," I said, tugging Witte closer to my mentor-of-the-moment. "We just got married. June twentieth."

"My dear," Omar continued, directing his stogie breath toward Witte. "This Karcher of yours is a good man, to be so honest with his feelings. I'm going to help him. I said it then, and I'm saying it again. He's worth loving, worth holding onto." He eyed her closely. "I remember you. How could I forget such vigilant eyes? A figure like yours?"

Witte squirmed at the compliment, which was certainly not her normal reaction. Omar had penetrated more than her clothes. He seemed to sense the disquiet in her soul, to know the torment of mistrust she was experiencing.

It was not like Witte to give and regret. She committed to few things in life, and only after careful consideration. I was the first man, aside from Loring Murch, her father, that measured up. Loring had never let her down; I had. It was neither fading fervor nor waning allegiance but lost faith in her judgment that made Witte step back and blend with the crowd, leaving me alone to learn of my fate.

"Now, what can I do to help, Karcher?" Omar smiled reassuringly and leaned forward, so I didn't have to share my sensitive question with the world.

I studied the map of veins on the back of his hands, avoiding the scrutiny of his red, watery eyes, and began in a whisper. "I've become impotent. Since the wedding. It's not her fault. God, she's got more fire in her than all the boilers at the L. C. Andrew's mill. And, well, you can see how she's built." Tears welled in my eyes. "Omar, I love her so much. Why can't I let go?"

Omar patted my right hand between his palms. "Karcher, Karcher. You're not the first man to falter on his wedding night, believe me. Many a man has wilted before his new bride." He squeezed my hand. "It's the pressure, son."

"But you don't understand. Before, she was a chase. Now, she's become—I hate to admit it—*my* mother. Not just a mother figure—my mother. When she speaks, it's Nettie talking. When she gets undressed, it's my mom standing naked before me at night in the kitchen, brandishing the butcher knife she used to kill herself.

"It all started on the island. Christ, how I wish we'd gone to Hawaii, Niagara Falls—anywhere but there for our honeymoon.

"I think I'm going crazy, Omar. I mean, it's crazy to reject someone so devoted and gorgeous. When will I believe that Nettie is gone, that she has no more power over me? She's been dead for almost three years, for God's sake."

"Apparently not, Karcher, so far as you're concerned. Tell me, did you see her do it? Kill herself?"

"I didn't even get to her funeral. Hell, there *was* no funeral, just a memorial service with Dad and Bente, her last lover, the only ones present. I was away at college when it happened. Dad didn't even want me to come home."

Omar frowned and shook his head. "This is getting complicated, Karcher. Out of my league. You need professional help. I know a psychiatrist in Portland who might be willing to see you. Her name is Auburn Locke. L-O-C-K-E, like the lawn mower. I think you should give her a ring."

Now it was my turn to shudder. I hated psychiatrists, those faceless quacks entrusted to cure my mother, those 'worse than useless' mind manipulators who took Dad's money, twisted Nettie's brain further, and then sent her home to commit suicide. If a hospital team of them in Connecticut was that incompetent, imagine the damage a lone one from the rural State of Maine could do to a patient. Besides, I was no patient. I didn't need a doctor.

Furious, I turned away, and regained Witte in the crowd. "You know what Omar suggested?" I blurted. "That I see a psychiatrist. Not just any psychiatrist, mind you, but a woman named Locke. A *woman*. Can you imagine? Me, the patient of a *woman* doctor?"

Witte's eyes narrowed, and her jaw set hard. Between clenched teeth, she hissed: "Sick of women, are you? Nettie. Bente. Now Doctor Locke. And me?"

Only the irises of her eyes were visible now, bituminous with rage and fixed on mine. "Tell you what, Engine Boy. Go back to your Fairbanks-Morse Wilbur and your other tired iron friends. I'll just pretend this little union never took place. You want freedom? You got it."

Witte snapped an about-face and stormed for shore. I stood for a moment, dumbfounded, watching her roily silk swish with each thrust of her powerful stride, like a proud Arabian filly gating before her judges. No, I thought, as I listened to the hammer of her heels fade from the pier planks, this woman is not like the rest. She's almost an engine, and badly in need of servicing.

I'd never have neglected Wilbur, my favorite one-lunger, like this. I made sure to oil him so he wouldn't squeal, to choke him gingerly so he wouldn't flood, to etch his hopper with acid before the calcium deposits caused him to overheat, to warm his tub water on winter mornings, and wait until he was up to temperature before switching his diet from gasoline to kerosene, so he wouldn't cough. I felt his pulse, took his temperature, wiped up his spills, adjusted his mixture when he complained, and gave him a kerosene rub down at the end of a hard day. I kept Wilbur content. Why couldn't I do that for Witte?

I found Witte by the carousel, standing next to the canopy post in front of the Wurlitzer 157 Military Band organ that had moved me to tears those many summer nights during our courtship. It was playing Irving Berlin's "What Does It Matter?", and this time Witte was crying.

When I came within the field of her broad, blurred focus, she slowly turned toward me. Her prominent dark eyebrows, pinched with anguish, looked black against the pallor of her long oval face. Her eyes, now capacious crucibles of molten steel, were pouring, imploring. Gone from her frame was the rigid shield of defiance. Gone too was the plucky, pert cock of her head, the crisp delivery of her lines. It seemed to take all the wind she had, to sob over her protruding lower lip, "Th...that's our waltz, K...Karcher." She held out a quaking, milk-white hand to me across the boardwalk. "Dance w...with me, dear."

I looked in vain to Vernon, the carousel's operator, for a cue, but he continued to stare vacantly from the controls of his empty ride, while the organ kept yammering, verse after verse:

What does it matter if the sun won't shine,
'Long as you are mine; what does it matter?

What does it matter if the clouds appear,
'Long as you are near; what does it matter?

Life is never one sweet song;
Things are liable to go wrong.
What does it matter, 'long as I love you,
And you love me too; what does it matter?

Troubles and worries may darken the day.
Shadows may frighten the sunshine away.
Winds may blow over the land and the sea.
But as long as there's you and there's me,
What does it matter?

Incredulous, I turned to Witte. "What, here?"
"S...sure. What've w...we got t...to lose?"
She extended both her arms, and I reluctantly moved toward her. When I got within range of her scent, my iron will melted, and we fell together, clutching one another as much for support as for forgiveness, our heads buried in each other's neck to avoid the pain of close scrutiny.

Vernon saw us start to sway, and kicked the roll into rewind to repeat the number. The organ paused on a minor chord, howled its protest at the interruption, swapped rolls and blared the first few bars of Sousa's "Liberty Bell," quit again, growling low C on the trombone, then shifted back to the rewound roll. For a few seconds, all we heard was the sinister throb of the pump rods slapping their journals: "Ticka-tacka, ticka-tacka, ticka-tacka...." as the blank leader ran past the tracker bar. Then the waltz opened with its tragic descending chromatic scale.

It was at moments like this, infrequent as they had been with such a secure partner, that I could feel the steadying hand of self-control, just a tinge of power. Witte's falter allowed me a brief moment in the sun. It was the recognition of being needed by one who for the moment was more wretched than myself.

There were many times, of course, when my parents had been in a weaker state than I, but they never asked for my help. It was always a doctor, or someone old and wise who would be called in to dispense advice, moral support or first aid. I wasn't to be trusted with such delicate matters. And so I remained always 'worse than useless' to them.

Here with Witte I could take charge, but the obvious response did not come easily to me. There was the fear that Witte would suddenly become strong again, like Nettie, and beat back my ego to age seven. If I could just keep her weak and needy in my arms like this forever, I'd be all right.

Like all human relationships, I knew that control through weakness was precarious and tenuous at best; it couldn't be depended upon. But over-designed, low pressure engines like Wilbur and the Wurlitzer could. From them I could always draw strength. At this moment I was lucky to have both: Witte weak in my arms and the organ beating in time with my heart.

Still locked in her embrace, I began to lead. Gradually, Witte filled her chest, straightened and drew away until she was weightless under my fingers, gliding before me without apparent guidance like a well-oiled and fully wound clockwork automaton. The tarred and separated fir boardwalk planks which would have tripped an ordinary mortal became a shimmering maple dance floor under our feet, the carousel a stage full of mighty musicians playing just for us, the blur of colored lights and flashing mirrors a slowly turning, crystalline globe scattering dots of light about our now darkened and infinite ballroom. For a precious few moments this unbounded, singular backdrop floated in my imagination as I gazed into Witte's huge, hypnotic eyes.

But what I saw there was more than a fantastic illusion. Deep within her eyes I saw my soul, and it surprised me to discover that the core of Karcher was not a lifeless lump of coal, but a vital source of sustaining energy, a perpetual furnace of healing power there for the tapping. I would need to draw upon that strength many times in the months ahead, as indeed I must have in the past without knowing it.

Like most insights, it was gone as soon as I experienced it. As my focus pulled back from infinity, the portrait before me grew tangible but no less lovely.

Chapter 3

AUBURN

"Karcher, dear, pass me that light so I can see this place." I handed Witte the drop light to inspect our first home, a rented brick basement flat on Pine Street in Portland. Though it was nearly noon in mid July, the apartment I'd secured for us was dim as a dungeon. As Witte moved the light about the two empty rooms, her eyes scanned with the distant focus of resignation. When she was through, she hooked the light on a nail, slumped against the bathroom door frame and sighed. "I thought my barracks at the Beach was gloomy."

"It's better than a tent," I said, fingering the curled corner of Formica on the kitchen counter. "And you don't have to pump water and burn kerosene to cook and see at night."

Witte stiffened. Her eyes stopped to slits, and her jaw muscles bulged with the clamping. "I'm *not* a slicker. Don't need amenities, just a breath of air and a window facing west."

"I was only kidding. Knowing you, you'll turn this cell into a palace within a week. Come on, let's get the gear aboard."

We both knew it was all we could afford in town. The Varney Grange had collected a hundred dollars for our wedding present, and we'd gone through some of that already. My Model A Ford was on its last legs, too decrepit to reliably ferry us to work from the country. And although Witte's parents had offered to put us up until we could afford decent digs, we needed privacy, and so said no. Witte found work singing at DeMillo's on the waterfront, and I became an engineer's assistant at Portland Copper and Tank across the bridge. Together we brought home a hundred and fifty a week, sometimes more when Witte entertained an office party. It was a start.

As it turned out, our financial stability was never in question. It was our emotional state—or, rather, mine—that needed governing. Even here, in the city, I was unable to banish Nettie's ghost from our home—advising, scolding, threatening. I tried to cover my anxiety by filling every waking moment off work with kinetic activity: helping Witte fix up the apartment, tinkering with my Ford, jogging along the waterfront. I even dragged Witte to a square dance class on Thursday evenings. Every weekend Witte was off and the Model A was willing, we'd visit her folks, dance at the Grange and help around the farm. The ploy was largely successful so long as I remained conscious, but I risked losing control of my mind when I slept, so I started drinking coffee to stay awake. As my system adapted to the caffeine, I had to keep increasing the dose, until I was up to eight or nine cups a day, at which point my stomach could no longer differentiate between coffee nerves and an anxiety attack. Besides, I had become so fatigued from getting three to four hours of sleep a night that prolonged coma was finally inevitable, allowing Nettie to visit my dreams and get in "a few good kicks," as Hiram, her father, used to say.

Part of the urge to maintain productive activity was also Nettie's doing. As a child, I was accused of being "a lazy lout" whenever I paused to rest. In my late teens, I was "tootling around" whenever I used the family car for any activity that didn't benefit her. And woe betide me if I lost my job or flunked a college course because I "frittered time" on "trivialities."

When sleeping, of course, I wasn't "gainfully employed," and my system knew it. If I was lucky, I would wake before I got so nauseous that I would lose my supper. Then I could dash out into the night air—the colder and breezier, the better—and heave deep breaths before it was too late. I had become deathly afraid of vomiting. It was a sure sign of losing control, but at the time I had no idea of the connection, only that I must keep down my supper at all costs. Sometimes a dream would wake me, usually a life-threatening chase scene where my assailant—often a giant steam locomotive, a great horned owl, or a composite of my grade school peers, twice my size and menacing me with their fists—was gaining on me, and I was never able to dodge, dive or otherwise divert from a predetermined path, as if walled into a maze.

Witte, usually a sound sleeper, would be roused by my thrashing and groaning and have my sedative—the balance of Nettie's phenobarbital, which would run out soon—and water ready. I'd awaken to her drawn and imploring face, suffocatingly close to mine, whispering away my oxygen with "Simmer down, dear. She can't hurt you anymore," or words to that effect. Logic and proximity at such moments were just the wrong medicine. I'd push her away, sit up, gasp for air and quickly evaluate the progress of my panic. Had I caught it early enough to suppress the nausea with fresh air alone? If not, was there time for the phenobarb to take effect, and how many grains would it take to knock me out? Was this a fairly mild, three-grain attack or a full-blown five-grainer? Or was it so advanced that I needed to dash for the toilet?

After weathering five or six episodes of midnight nursing—holding my head over the toilet, mopping my brow with a moistened wash cloth, fanning me with shirt cardboard, then pacing away the wee hours of a workday morning with me, repeatedly circumnavigating our tiny flat until the drug took hold—Witte put her foot down. "Karcher," she announced when I returned at two a.m. from streaking through the neighborhood in my pajamas to quell a mild attack, "You've got to get help—professional help. I can't take this any more.

"You're missing work. You look grave as a ghost. We haven't made love in weeks. It isn't natural."

"That's not true," I said. "What about the night of July 4th, when we got the key to that bungalow?"

"Oh, you mean the night you slept on the floor, 'cause you felt ashamed at how long it took you to come? I about had to break you in two. And what did I get out of it? A charley horse in my right arm."

"I told you, you should have switched hands." I tried to keep a straight face, but Witte was in no mood for joking.

My spell had passed, and I was becoming concupiscent—just impish at first. Then, as I grew more confident and began to act my age, lust replaced the little devil in me. For the first time since our rumble in the Grange band closet during the Thanksgiving dance, I felt like making love to Witte.

It was then nearly three on Tuesday morning. Witte had worked until nine and had copped barely four hours sleep. It wasn't wise to try to seduce her on an empty stomach. She became brittle and snapped like a hypoglycemic at such times. And here she'd had more than a deficiency of calories to irritate her.

"You got a lot of Moxie teasin' at this hour. If you're up to fooling around, you're well enough to sleep. We'll discuss your therapy in the morning. Now, get some rest." With that, she switched off the light, dove under the covers and faced away from me.

"My therapy?" I put on the light. "You know how I feel about therapists. I'll handle my own problems, thank you."

As soon as I said it, I knew it was nonsense. I wasn't in control at all. But this spell was over, and I wanted to make love.

"I know your problem," I continued softly in her exposed ear. "You're hungry. You always get testy on an empty stomach. I'll fix you a toasted muffin and milk. Won't take me a minute."

Witte exhausted most of the air in her lungs before answering. "*Men* get testy; women get exasperated with men." Her last word—men—was expelled like the final thrust of a dying dowager.

Good, I thought, stealing away to the kitchen. She's not beyond recall. There's a spark in her yet, even at this hour. I tore open a sack of Thomas's English Muffins—Witte would accept no substitute—and forked one apart, stabbing myself in the process. Between drags on my bleeding thumb, I managed to spill the milk and get the thick half of the muffin stuck in the toaster. By the time I returned to the bedroom with the overdone thin half and milk, she was asleep.

Witte was sprawled across our new queen-size bed on her back. It appeared she'd been tossing, as her hair was splashed over the expanse of white percale and her hands were resting beside her head. I set the muffin and milk on the night stand and stood awhile, watching her sleep, transfixed by her stoic smile. She had resolved to confront our problem with me in the morning. Until then, she would sleep undisturbed. There was no other way with her, and I could not bear to break her trust.

Feeling faintly hungry myself, I ate her snack and edged into bed, gently gathering her hair that had fallen on my pillow and letting it slide through my fingers into a neat bundle alongside her cheek. Soon I too was asleep.

* * * * * * * *

I never heard the alarm, but there was no chance I'd oversleep. Witte waved a mug of strong coffee under my nose and firmly depressed the mattress next to my shoulder with her derriere.

"Mornin', dear," she almost commanded in my ear. "It's nearly seven. We've got to talk."

Groggy as I was, I could tell by the tone of her voice that she was all business. And though her proximate posterior begged to be pinched, I dared not lay a hand on it, or any other projection of hers within reach. To be sure I didn't touch her, even inadvertently, I rolled away onto my back and stretched carefully. "Grrraw! What time did you say it was?"

"Five of seven."

I was handed the mug before I could get to a seated position. Witte turned to face me and drew one leg under her, exposing its shapely calf.

"Now, I want you to concentrate on what I have to say."

Using my heels and elbows, I wriggled toward the headboard, juggling the steaming mug from hand to hand until I could elevate my head sufficiently to sip without choking.

Witte looked ripe for a tumble in her abbreviated flannel nightshirt. Her hair was unrestrained, and so apparently were her breasts. It was all I could do to restrain myself from wrestling her to the sheets. But her cold gray eyes kept me in check. She had a lot to say, and I suffered it and sipped.

"Last night was your final audition, Karcher. As your producer, I get to evaluate your performance, and the time has come for that accounting." She paused to allow the analogy to sink in.

"My verdict? You're a lousy actor." Her lower lip drew up, the corners of her mouth drooped, and her chin jutted. It was Loring speaking, except that Witte didn't tip her head from side to side as her father did when delivering such lines.

"Unless you submit to professional coaching and show improvement, our contract will be terminated. It's not my job, nor do I have the skills, to straighten you out." She broke eye contact and looked down.

"Karcher, I don't like talking to you this way. But I'm frazzled, fresh out of ideas. I've tried to understand, nurse you, and sub for your mother when you regress. But it's no good. It's driving a wedge between us." Her eyes, now large and pale, returned to mine.

"It's necessary that you see someone, dear. A doctor who can prescribe medicine. You're almost out of sedative." She drew a quick breath and exhausted a shaky sigh.

"Truth is, Karcher, I'm scared. I thought I could handle it. I never told you...." She looked down again, plaintively, like a girl of nine about to admit an indiscretion to her grandfather.

"Daddy took me aside after supper last May. Said he didn't want to trouble Mumma with his ruminatin'. You know how he gets when he's het up. Well, he took me aside and told me he was worried about your mental stability. Didn't want me to 'tie myself to an emotional cripple,' he said. I 'deserve a solid man to lean on, not some alder sapling that buckles in a breeze.' He'd seen you cry, and was afraid you'd inherited weakness from your folks." Witte shuddered, then lifted her eyes once more to search mine.

"He likes you, Karcher. Very much. You know that." I saw her eyes begin to fill and reached for her, but she drew back and stiffened. Her lips pursed and her forehead furrowed.

"Daddy had a point. I don't want him to be right.

"Now, you have a reference from Omar, a Dr. Locke, here in town. It's a start. I want you to see her, and the sooner the better."

"But she's a woman, and a psychiatrist."

"And what's wrong with a woman being a doctor?"

"I'm sure that's fine for most patients, but I've been bossed by a woman all my life. I don't want to be at the business end of a woman's rifle any more. Anyway, psychiatrists shouldn't call themselves doctors. They're just fumbling in the dark, like the rest of us, only they're getting rich."

"Maybe so, but we've got to start somewhere. Perhaps Dr. Locke could recommend a male therapist for you. I want you to call her today." Witte had finished and stood to dress.

With her weight removed, the bed leveled. My command of the mattress and the distance now between us gave me courage to object more strenuously.

"You know, you're getting to sound more like Nettie every day. I can just hear this Dr. Locke now. 'It's quite common, Mr. Stickney, for a man to marry someone like his mother—a replacement, to continue his care.' Lovely, just lovely. I'm a mental cripple and need continued mothering. No wonder I agreed so quickly to marry you."

"You didn't agree that easy, as I remember," came a low voice from the bathroom.

I had forgotten how hard I'd fought Witte's proposal announcement. It was issued as a warning. "I think we better get married," was how she phrased it the morning after my wet dream in her bungalow, as if it might be too late if we waited or didn't. I had run through all the reasons why I shouldn't get tied to another woman, but none of them applied to Witte then. Now I wasn't so sure.

* * * * * * * *

Going to a psychiatrist was out of the question I told myself confidently while staring past the drawing of a compressor casting on my desk (where I was supposed to be brainstorming how to cut the cost of the thing without weakening it—Value Engineering, they called it). We couldn't afford it. It was that simple, but I didn't dare throw that argument up to Witte; she might think of a way around our insolvency, like using my company's health insurance, which paid half the cost of all sessions for up to a year. I certainly didn't want to risk divulging any psychological weakness at work by applying for insurance. Besides, there was no way I was going to get help from some quack woman doctor telling me where to get off. I already had a wife running my life.

No, that's unfair, I thought, the thin ozalid lines of the drawing a blur before me. Witte was simply stating the obvious. She was capable of neither exaggeration nor understatement, and was just trying to save our marriage. Nettie, by contrast, had manipulated the truth.

About eleven o'clock, I gave up trying to concentrate, and went to the pay phone outside the lunchroom. I opened the phone book to L and flipped though the listings: Lancaster...Leffingwell...Locke, Auburn K., MD., 1

Dana Street. My heart began palpitating, and my hand shook so, I could barely insert the dime.

"Dr. Locke's office," came a smoky contralto on the line. I expected a woman to answer, but I wasn't prepared for the earthy gravity of the voice I heard: Tallulah Bankhead with a Maine accent.

"Hi. Um. I wanted to make an appointment to discuss a possible course of therapy." I couldn't believe I was asking. "Are you Dr. Locke, by chance?"

"I am. And your name, sir?"

"Karcher Stickney. I live in town. How soon could we get together? I'm rather apprehensive about this."

"How would tomorrow afternoon at three fit with your schedule? I assume you work days. Could you get free tomorrow?"

"I...I think so. If I have a problem, I'll call back. Let's see, Dana Street is near the waterfront, isn't it?"

"Yes. It tees into Commercial Street between Exchange and High. My office is in the basement. Use the side door. See you at three tomorrow. Bye." She hung up before I could thank her.

I returned to the sea of white shirts to find my boss, Dorrance Dillman, hunched over the drawing on my desk. "Getting anywhere with this, Karch?" I hadn't laid a line on the paper.

"Uh, n...no, not yet. Say, Dory, I have a doctor's appointment at three tomorrow. I should be back by four fifteen."

"Good enough."

Dory was a man of few words, like Loring—just the right prescription for a supervisor. And although I'd been on the job only a couple of months, he seemed to trust me. I was counting on him to ask no questions, and he didn't let me down.

* * * * * * * *

Witte lifted her eyes from the stove but made no move to embrace me when I came in. "Huy," she said softly.

"I'm going tomorrow," I said, keeping my distance and looking at her shoes.

I barely heard her inhaled reply, "Yuh."

Witte made no further remarks until supper was over. When she'd swallowed her last morsel of haddock, she tried again. "I know it took guts to call that woman, Karcher." Her delivery sounded more like a question of survival than a compliment. My impression was confirmed by the cant of her head and the torment I saw in her eyes. It was the rare look she gave me when she was unsure of her position, one that begged forgiveness before her words were spilled. I knew she was trying to hold us together. It just wouldn't be fair to tell her how I really felt.

"You're always so understanding," I said. "I love you for that, and much, much more, as you know."

Witte stood with our plates in her hands. "We'll see."

"I'll do the dishes, Witte," I said, jumping up to take the plates from her. "You better get dressed, or you'll be late for work."

I'd just finished setting the plates on the counter when I felt a kiss on my nape. But when I turned to acknowledge it, she had left the room. Less than five minutes later, she reappeared in her rose satin cocktail dress and matching pumps, pecked me on the cheek and dashed for the door, leaving me reeling at the sink in a cloud of Chanel Russia Leather.

* * * * * * * *

Dana Street, spanning just two blocks, was paved with cobble stones, and the old brick buildings along it looked like they'd been there almost as long. The ship chandlery mid street still had parts for my favorite marine engine, the one-cylinder Universal Fisherman. Its ancient bay windows, brimming with bronze fittings, foul weather suits and charts were a welcome sight as I descended the hill to number one. I let myself in through a low door which led down seven steps to the basement. The place had a pungent, old factory odor of oil-soaked yellow pine and raw iron. My footsteps echoed as I traversed the corridor of gated bins and transomed offices with stenciled windows looking inward. A sign on the door under Dr. Locke's shingle read: PLEASE REFRAIN FROM KNOCKING. ENTER AND HAVE A SEAT IN THE LOBBY. I'LL BE WITH YOU SHORTLY.

I slipped inside the waiting room and settled in one of the two chairs. In one corner, beside a clogged and sparking electrostatic precipitator trying to cope with a pall of cigarette smoke, stood a small table. On it was an open jar of potpourri, an overfull ash tray and several dog-eared issues of *Psychology Today*. I picked up a copy, opened it and stared, glassy eyed past the print. Through the open transom, I heard a soothing voice from the next room. Although too muffled to decipher, it sent waves of tranquility up and down my spine. Perhaps coming here wasn't such a bad idea after all.

Louder voices, two of them now, emanated from the closed room, then the door opened. A young woman emerged, drying her eyes. She shuffled silently to the door, sniffling into her handkerchief, and left.

"Won't you come in," crooned the tall redhead filling the open inner office doorway. "You must be Karcher Stickney." She extended a warm and fleshy, freckled hand, which I shook tentatively.

"Hi," I said, trying to avoid her china blue eyes. "Dr. Locke?"

"Uh-huh. Have any trouble finding me?"

"N...no. Your directions were fine, thank you."

The room was barely big enough to accommodate the couch, two stuffed chairs, a cassette recording console and the two of us.

"Why don't you just get comfy while I grab a pad," she said with a disarming smile. She breezed into the hall and returned with a notepad and pencil, kicked off her loafers and settled into the larger of the two chairs. I dropped to the edge of the sofa farthest from her. "Let's start with a little history, shall we?"

Dr. Locke crafted her interrogation so innocuously, I found myself divulging much more of my past in twenty minutes than I had to Witte in as many months. Her syrupy voice had a hypnotic effect that allowed me to sketch my rawest childhood traumas without the slightest anxiety. I became so enthralled, I completely forgot to recite my opening plea for a reduced fee.

Auburn Locke had more than just a mesmerizing voice. There was a personal intensity to her approach that seemed more than professional, as if I were her only patient.

"And so you quite naturally turned to inanimate objects for solace, even friendship," she concluded. "Your human role models, your parents, were unable to provide the foundation for your ego development." She paused. "Are you following me, Karcher?"

"Yes, I think so."

"Good. We'll examine this role breakdown and the effect it has had on you in greater detail next time. For now, let's discuss what it is you want to accomplish in therapy and whether I can be of help."

"You already have," I blurted, noticing how her hair fell in soft ringlets about her broad shoulders, how the patina of her freckles-in-cream complexion complemented the cushiony curves of her body. Judging by the distended veins in her hands and the fine creases radiating from her eyes, I guessed her age to be a bit over thirty-five.

I told her of my anxiety attacks, of my love for Witte and my frustration at being so often angry and impotent with her. She suggested a program of hypnosis to 'painlessly break through the facade shielding your naked ego.' Once the embryo ego inside me learned to trust a friendly intruder, she promised, it would gain the strength to change misperceptions into constructive opportunities.

The thought of painless healing in the hands of this magical mother had already banished the negative thoughts I'd held about psychotherapy and those who practiced the art. But Auburn's gracious understanding of my flimsy finances was the clincher. She agreed to see me once a week for ten dollars a session, a third of her normal fee. I left a new man, made over in just fifty minutes.

* * * * * * *

It was too easy. I knew it the moment I set foot in our apartment.

Wednesday was Witte's day off. She greeted me at the door wrapped in her white terry robe, fresh from the shower and simpering seductively. "How'd it go, dear? Tell me everything. Was she nice?"

My ego, which had finally surpassed age seven, shrank to a speck that swam in a viscous, acoustically damped amniotic fluid. Witte's words became distorted and distant, reverberating and ringing as if they had been uttered from the bottom of a granite well.

"What did you say?" I asked, trying to shake the cacophony from my head. I stepped inside and closed the door behind me.

Witte didn't answer me right away, but slipped the knot that cinched the robe around her slender waist, let the folds fall open and wrapped the toweling around me as she drew me to her. Although at five-six, only a few inches shorter than my stately doctor, Witte's body, by contrast, resembled that of a spider, all arms and legs radiating from an hourglass torso. There was suddenly not enough of her in my arms. Repulsed, I pulled back.

"That bad, Karcher?"

"She was very helpful," I interjected quickly, "but I'm not supposed to discuss it with anyone. Dr. Locke said it would weaken the impact, confuse my assimilation. I'm supposed to just let it soak in and deal with the feelings that come up. If I get uncomfortable or have questions, she said to call her."

"I see." Witte's small mouth firmed. She drew the robe about her and retied the sash with a jerk. "Supper's in ten minutes. You must be starved."

We ate and passed the evening without further conversation. Witte darned my socks on the couch while listening to oldies on WGAN. I read Audel's Engine Manual in Nettie's wing chair, which I'd scavenged from our converted barn in Connecticut before it was sold. Every now and then I'd feel Witte's eyes on me. I avoided them like a guilty child, sneaking a furtive glance at her only when I was sure she was looking at her work. About ten, I headed for the shower.

"I'm going to hit the sack," I called from the bedroom. "The alarm's set for six. Night."

"I'll be in, in a minute."

From my cozy fetal position I heard the distant clatter of dishes being replaced in the cupboard followed by little feet padding to the bathroom. A hiss from the toilet, abruptly interrupted several times by silence. (Kegels—I should be grateful.) The flush. Now water running in the sink. I braced for the inevitable staccato strokes of plastic against porcelain. (Witte habitually inertia-dried her toothbrush by repeatedly striking it against the sink). A pileated woodpecker was no match for the impact of this woman. It was her final act before bed and the last I heard from her each morning as I went out the door.

It was over. I relaxed. The bathroom light went out. More padding. The robe fell away, and Witte's soft, warm body nuzzled against me under the covers.

"Karcher, dear, you must be about ready to burst after all this time. It's been three, two weeks, at least."

"I'm fine," I said, flipping over to face her but maintaining my fetal tuck.

"No, you're not," she cooed. "I can tell when your plumbing's congested." She began stroking my exposed right testicle with her index fingernail.

"Can't you let a man get some sleep?"

"No."

She flashed a wicked grin and disappeared under the covers. It didn't take her long to convince me she had correctly sized up the situation. Witte commanded an arsenal of persuasion tactics, and I responded in spite of myself.

Chapter 4

TINDER

The gibbous October moon was a silver smudge in the east at midnight on Saturday when Witte and I left the Varney Grange and climbed into the Model A. Weary dancers drifting from the drafty, hipped-roof Adam, clustered to farewell then dispersed to their cars.

"Fixin' to storm," Loring called from the back stoop. "Tomorrow night, I figure," he added, gesturing toward the moon with his free hand, the other clutching a sheaf of sheet music from the twenties. "Good night, lovebirds." He waved and began his descent of the ten steep steps, clutching the bannister and rocking his head from side to side, as he did when things were unsettled.

I heard a small, sleepy voice beside me croak, "We better get wood in the morning, dear." Witte was so accustomed to her father's reasoning that his mere mention of a storm brewing triggered the appropriate response. I was tempted to remind her that she now lived in a steam-heated apartment, but it was late and she was on home turf.

"For the fireplace," I said, steering her back to reality. She yawned and curled up against me. I nudged the Klaxon and let out the clutch. The Model A lurched forward, teeter-turned right on the apron and chuffled east on Route 22.

* * * * * * * *

Sunday dawned the color of Witte's eyes. An east wind had blown the fog in early. Our bedroom was raw as a schooner's cabin at sunup. I pulled the blanket around me as I left the bed to shut the window. Witte, not yet fully awake, drew herself into a ball under the sheet, murmuring unintelligible expletives. I shuffled into the living room and thumbed the thermostat. When I returned, Witte was standing naked at parade rest in the doorway, glowering.

"I may be warm blooded, but even a country girl needs beddin'."

"Then put some clothes on."

My vision blurred. Instead of Witte, I saw Nettie, naked, blocking my entry to her kitchen, where she had been sharpening her Hoffritz.

"For God's sake, woman. Get dressed."

I broke into a cold sweat. Witte didn't budge, and neither did Nettie. Without thinking, I tore the blanket off and threw it over the woman in front of me. There was a brief struggle and more muffled expletives while the blanket was rearranged about her shoulders.

"Least you could wait till I've had coffee before you start a row."

"I'm...I'm sorry. I thought..."

Witte raised an eyebrow. "He looks a mite chilly, dear."

"Oh, jeeez." The realization that I was now naked, completely cleared my head of Nettie, and I bolted for the shower.

It was going to be another Sunday game of chess, but this time I decided not to play. Let her get the wood, I thought, if she wants a fire. Today I'm cruising the island circuit, fog or no fog. She can fend for herself.

"It's time we put some miles between us," I announced confidently at breakfast. "I'm taking the noon ferry. You can use the Model A to visit your folks and get wood. We'll meet back here for supper at six."

Witte put down her fork and looked up from her eggs. Her eyes searched my face as if she didn't know me. "Never, ever, have I heard you ask to be alone." She smiled. "You *have* been getting help from Dr. Locke."

"I'll pull out the backseat cushion before I go. Just throw an army blanket over the seat back and load the wood carefully, no higher than the windowsills."

Witte stood, drew a deep breath, shot me a salute and winked. "Aye, aye, Captain." Then she sat down to finish her breakfast. She wasn't about to let me leave without a reminder of what I'd be missing.

* * * * * * * *

Casco Bay Lines was having a bad Sunday. Tourists for the most part stayed away from the sea when it was foggy. They missed the best cruises.

On murky days, the water was usually calm. Sea sounds rang and echoed with unusual clarity but without direction. As the ferry slipped along, the hoary haze shrouding the islands now and then parted, revealing hunched figures fishing from jetties and gulls perching silently in flocks a safe distance away, all facing in the same direction. People aboard the ferry spoke in hushed tones and understood one another perfectly. You got closest to the sea and self on days like this. It was the perfect setting for mulling over my marriage.

Leaving our apartment, I strolled down High, along Commercial, and out along the pier that supported Boone's restaurant, arriving at the gate just as it was to be chained. Most of the passengers were already inside the cabin when I stepped aboard and made my way to the foredeck.

From the eyes of the ferry I could take command. Without shelter and with only the sea ahead of me, nothing escaped my scrutiny: the shape of an advancing swell; the proximity of a looming weir; the flicker of a channel marker's lantern; the knell of a buoy's gong. There I could ride the surge of my vessel, gauge its response and steer it clear of danger.

I had only to turn around to capture the majesty of her power: eighty feet and twenty tons, obediently following, lights glowing in her cabin under the darkened bridge. Beneath me, her timbers throbbed to the resolute pulse of her Kahlenberg diesel poking holes in the mist with an endless procession of smoke donuts.

For the first time since Nettie died, I was enjoying solitude. The confusion of relationships ashore—with Witte, with Auburn Locke and with my boss, Dory—seemed inconsequential out here. I felt in control. Even Nettie seemed to have lost her power over me. If I stayed alone at sea, I reasoned, anxiety couldn't get a toehold. There would be no need for therapy.

A twinge in my solar plexus reminded me that life at sea wasn't a permanent solution to my discomfort. Even a captain—which for a moment I fantasized becoming—must spend time in port interacting with others. And I sensed that loneliness would soon obliterate inner peace, replacing panic with despair. I could wind up in the sea for good, a victim of my escape.

Of course, there was no escaping from myself. As long as these recordings of inadequacy were lodged in my brain, I would react according to their instruction, which was to mistrust everyone I encountered, most of all myself. It mattered little where I was. Once the tape was triggered and rolling, my place in humanity became unclear.

The tapes had to be erased and new recordings made that built self-worth. Dr. Locke had set a sensible goal for my rehabilitation. All I had to do was cooperate with her course of therapy, and in time my brain would be reprogrammed. While that required trust—normally an impossible posture for me—with her, I found submission less threatening, almost seductive. If anyone could cure me, it was Auburn Locke.

* * * * * * * *

Without bothering to shower, Witte tugged on a pair of overaged and undersized dungarees, then her work boots, and wriggled into her bulky green ragg wool sweater one arm at a time while racking the breakfast dishes with her free hand. She filled the watering can, grabbed the ignition key, and two army blankets from the chest, and headed for the car. After topping up the radiator, she lifted the right half of the hood, cocked her head to clear her vision, puffed away the remaining strands of hair from her eyes, then pried the water pump packing nut until it stopped dripping. Satisfied, she lowered the hood and reset its latches. Before sliding behind the wheel, she took charge of her unruly tresses by snapping them into a pony tail with an elastic.

Spark up, gas down two notches, mixture rich one-half, choke drawn, ignition cylinder popped, starter tromped, choke rod dropped at first fire, spark down—Witte ran through the starting drill with such dispatch that an old-timer on foot stopped to admire her. The man grinned at the shaking flivver, idling at the curb with its plucky driver. "Sounds pretty good, don't she?" he shrieked with delight.

Witte shook her head. "She's gettin' awful tired." She cranked the wheel over and pulled ahead into traffic, leaving a staccato trail of blue exhaust and a burst of rod rattle for the gent to savor.

A half mile west of the city on Route 22 the A emerged from the fog under a lowering blanket of clouds. Witte shoved the bottom of the windshield forward to help clear the oily haze building up in the cabin. When the Ford started to rap on an upgrade, she backed off the throttle and nudged the spark up a notch or two, to ease it over the crest. In the flats, she pulled her foot off the accelerator and drove with the hand throttle, which was easier to modulate with the jouncing.

The idea of taking wood from her dad wasn't setting right. Well she knew the work of laying in a winter's supply of fuel, having loaded countless cords of "piss" oak splits falling from her father's maul into the truck, driven the teetering load to the barn, and stacked the fetid sticks to the rafters, three at a time, since she was little heavier than her burden. Loring didn't have a son to help with the chores, and his wife, Ida, was usually too busy in the kitchen to help. Now Loring had to do the work mostly alone.

He'd have given her the wood; it was only a few pieces. But they were to be burned in an inefficient, open fireplace. She couldn't stand to see her dad wince at the waste. It wasn't fair to put him through that. She'd buy the wood from a sawyer before visiting her folks. They needn't even know about it.

Witte remembered seeing a sign advertising cord wood for sale along Route 22, on the right, before the church at the intersection of Broad Turn. She slowed the A and scanned the shoulder. The sign was still there, nailed to a post marking the entrance to a gravel fire road. She nosed the Ford into the rutted lane. After winding a half mile through the alders, the road broke into the open, crossed a field and climbed a short rise to a dilapidated farmhouse at the edge of a wood lot, where it ended in a slough. Beside the barn, a brawny man in a red and black checked wool shirt was feeding oak to a saw rig. Witte stopped alongside a pile of seasoned splits and got out.

The man took note of his visitor, made the final two cuts on the stick and let the table rock back empty. Across the valley rang the mournful knell of tempered steel crying relief. The old six-horse Fairbanks-Morse one-lunger recovered with a crescendo of cannon reports, then closed its throttle and settled down to honking and thumping contentedly while the wide flat belt lashed and wove between the sheaves. As the man approached, all that was left of the saw's song was a hoarse hiss.

Witte met his gaze but held her ground. "Quarter cord should bring this heap about to her knees. How much?"

The sawyer rested a muddy boot on the Ford's running board just upwind of her. "Ain't you the Murch girl?" His voice was husky, and his overalls reeked of oak sap, sweat and grease.

"Name's Stickney. How much?"

"You don't remember me, do yuh?"

"Should I?" She flung open both back doors and started for the woodpile.

"I sat behind you in fifth grade. Third row. Waldron Weed. Folly Wally, you used to call me."

"Kid who kept blowing on my neck when I had my hair up?"

"Ayuh." Wally grinned broadly and joined Witte at the stack. "You sure growed up good."

Witte tried to ignore the tremor in her gut. "How much, Wally?"

"For you? Five bucks." He loaded a few sticks across her outstretched arms. "Got hitched, did yuh?"

"Yuh." Witte's inhaled reply was resigned, almost apologetic. "And you?"

Wally nodded, scooped up an armload and followed her to the Ford. "Parcy's due next month. Doctor says she has to rest, so it don't shake loose."

The Fairbanks gulped too much air and backfired.

Witte chuckled. "That engine sounds like my husband's. He got a Z like yours, only it's a newer model. Wilbur, he calls it, after the pig in *Charlotte's Web*. It's like a pet. Karcher's crazy over one-lungers." She frowned. "Seems I've got one lung too many."

"I'd hardly agree with him on that," Wally replied, raising an eyebrow.

Witte eyeballed him closely. "Now I remember why I called you Folly Wally. You was always angling for stuff out of reach." She paused. "You must have your hands full with a baby comin'."

"It sure stopped up the plumbin'. Parcy, she won't let me near her."

"Eight months? I should think not." Witte shook her head. "Shove s'more of this wood around, Wally. Then stick your head under the pump. If that don't work, run up and down the road." She raised her chin toward the house. "'Course, if she's a good woman, she'll drain you other ways."

Witte tried not to let Wally see the smirk on her face. She'd said far too much and felt suddenly as if she were looking down the muzzle of a loaded Smith & Wesson. She fumbled in her purse for a fiver and held it out to him. "Guess that's enough for this old girl."

Wally reached past the bill, grabbed Witte's hand and started to drag her toward him. "Not hardly, dear."

In a flash, Witte struck him a stinging blow across the face with her free hand. Wally let go and staggered back, rubbing his eyes. "Whoof. You've got more kick than my Z."

"Go make love to your engine, Wally. Can't you hear? She's pantin' for you up there." Witte gestured in disgust toward the huffing Fairbanks-Morse then bounced behind the wheel and tromped on the starter. The Ford caught on the second churn, crunched into gear and threw a clod of mud from its right rear tire before leaping forward in a tight arc. Witte cut the wheel back, popped into reverse, dug another divot, jammed it into first again and nearly ran over Wally's foot as he stood, gaping at the grown up little girl in the second row muscling her jalopy out of his grasp.

In the mirror, Witte saw Wally bend to scoop up the fiver that fluttered in the Ford's wake. He needed the money.

* * * * * * *

Loring Murch knew something was wrong the minute he caught sight of the Stickney sedan, down at the stern, wallowing over the ruts in his driveway, like a home bound Novi foundering in a following sea, before teetering to a halt back of the house. From the kitchen window he watched Witte pull the band from her hair, toss her locks into shape, get out, brush the chips from her sweater and stride through the dooryard. When she opened the door, he was filling the frame.

"Huy," she said softly, pecking her father on the cheek.

"You got Karcher boxed up with blocks back there to deep six?"

"Wish I'd thought of that." Witte brushed past him and into her mother's waiting arms, adding, "He's already at sea."

"Whatever are you two talking about?" Ida braced as if she were about to hear a murder confession.

"Karcher and I had words this morning, and he went off sailing." Witte paused. "Guess who I met this afternoon?"

"Now, just a minute," Loring barked. "What's goin' on between the two of you?"

"Not much. That's the trouble. He thinks I'm his mother."

Ida released the breath she'd been holding. "Well, dear, that sounds kinda nice." She winced. "His mother left him too early, and so suddenly. It's natural he'd want a substitute."

"That's applesauce, Ida, and you know it," Loring boomed. "What man wants to make love to his mother?"

"That's just it, Daddy. I can't 'rouse him much anymore. Ever since the wedding, he's been stuck on his mother. So, I got him to see a psychiatrist, and I think he's getting some help."

Seeing the blank look on her mother's face, Witte went into more detail. "See, Karcher's awful mad at his mother, and he's been taking it out on me."

Immediately, Witte regretted her wording. Her father was advancing and had started to chew his cud. Just the idea that someone would take advantage of his only daughter, made Loring bristle.

"Nothing physical, Daddy. He just don't want to be around me much."

Loring chomped loudly several times before he could get the words out. "It's time I had a talk with that boy. He needs to hear the truth, not some mumbo-jumbo from a quack."

"Give it a chance, Daddy. He's just getting comfortable with this woman, where he can open up to her."

"D'you say he's seeing another woman, Witte?" Loring's masticating now rivaled that of a rhinoceros, and his eyes were stopped to pencil points. "I won't have it," he roared, dropping his fist to the table.

Witte pulled a chair between her and her father and stood behind it, gripping the backrest for support. "Look, you don't understand. Dr. Locke is helping Karcher learn to accept what happened in his past and get on with his life. She's a licensed physician, Daddy."

"I don't care if she's the queen of England, I still don't like it. And just how much is this gander charging for her female intuition?"

"Ten dollars a week, Daddy. Don't worry, we're making the payments all right."

Loring shook his head. "You've always been a headstrong filly. Some day that's going to get you into a peck of trouble."

Ida, who had wisely stayed out of the line of fire, saw her chance to change the subject. "You were telling us about someone you met, dear."

Witte briefly related her meeting with Wally, discussing little about the wood and nothing about the pass he'd made at her. Loring had heard enough and stomped noisily from the kitchen to the woodshed. When he was gone, Witte moved closer to her mother and began in a low, husky voice: "It's not Dr. Locke I'm worried about. It's me. I was so mad at Karcher, I started flirtin' with Wally. He tried to grab me, and I whacked him. Please don't tell Daddy."

"What are you going to tell Karcher?"

"I don't know, Mumma. Nothin', I suppose. He wouldn't listen, anyway. He's too wrapped up in his own problems."

"They're your problems, too, Witte. If you want to make your marriage work—and it does take work—you'd better start talking to one another." Ida glanced at the Regulator above the range. "It's near four o'clock. You'd better get along. Don't let Karcher come home to an empty apartment."

Loring returned with an armload of birch and let it rumble into the kitchen wood box. "Better get that wood home before your struggle buggy collapses." He moved to the door.

Witte hastily took leave of her mother and left by the kitchen door. As she walked to the car, she noticed that her father was shadowing her. Without looking at him, she got behind the wheel and prepared the controls for starting the engine. When he let himself into the passenger seat and closed the door, she rolled her eyes heavenward and exhausted a sigh of exasperation. But Loring, wearing an uncharacteristic grin, didn't launch his expected lecture. "These Fords were popular with us kids," he began.

Witte's eyes remained cold as steel and fixed dead ahead.

"We had coupes," Loring continued, "so this feature came in handy for parking in the williwags." He gripped the gearshift, pulled up and swung its bent shaft around until the knob struck the dash. "Leg room for the ladies." He winked, let himself out and was gone.

Witte rotated the shifter back until its tang dropped into the slot, locking it in place. Struggle buggy indeed, she mused. I can just imagine Karcher's reaction to me pulling *that* stunt. Again, she felt that wanton tickle inside, like the flutter of a moth confined to her womb, and quickly drove the starter to the floor.

* * * * * * * *

Long before the ferry returned to its berth, the sea had drained my residual resentment and left tranquility in its wake.

It was five-thirty when I was greeted by a flickering fan of light penetrating the mist outside our apartment window. I stood on the sidewalk and followed the busy shadow to its source: Witte fixing supper. She had on one of my oxford shirts, its tails hiked and tied above her bare midriff, and a fresh pair of dungarees, no shoes. Her hair was wound up in a towel. Through the pantry door I could see a fire blazing on the living room hearth. The radio was blaring Perez Prado's "Patricia," and Witte was doing the mambo between the stove and sideboard.

When she heard the rattle of the lock, she lowered the radio volume and met me at the door with a coquettish curtsy, finishing by lifting her eyelids slowly until I felt the full weight of her stare. "Welcome home, Captain. How was your voyage?"

I closed the door behind me. The air in our narrow entry suddenly became saturated with the scent of the overheated woman facing me. Instinctively, I reached for the top button of her bursting blouse, but she drew her small hand there to block me. "Tsk, tsk," lisped her tiny pout, her head turned slightly aside, but her eyes implored for more.

The white terry turban smothering her hair focused attention on her delicate facial features, exaggerating the length of her neck and the size of her eyes. I took her narrow face in my hands and drew it to mine. There was no resistance. We stood, kissing softly without otherwise touching until neither of us could stand it any longer.

Supper waited until our passion was spent in front of the fire. There was a desperate urgency to Witte's lovemaking. And this time I did not let her down.

Chapter 5

TRUST

My sessions with Dr. Locke—twelve by mid November—had gone well. Hypnotherapy usually used up the first forty minutes, leaving a ten minute unwind and wrap up. Each time I left her office, the glow of self-assurance lasted a little longer before reality according to my subconscious tapes took over again. I was even able to experience moments of pleasure long after the euphoria wore off.

When first the power of my ego surfaced outside her office, it frightened me. I'd beat it back with fierce words of deprecation learned from Nettie. But by early November, I could no longer ignore the joy of feeling in control. Instead of dreading therapy each week, I began to crave it, which made me feel guilty around Witte, because our relationship seemed pale by comparison to my engagements with Auburn Locke.

The week before Thanksgiving, I swaggered to my appointment with a smirk. Auburn was late arriving, having run an errand that took longer than expected, and I had worked up a self-righteous grudge during my ten minute wait.

Sweetly, as always, she greeted me. "Karcher, forgive me. I know how frustrating it is to have to wait in an empty office. This needn't cut short our session. The gentleman I see after you, canceled. Please, come in." The velvet in her voice stroked my ego back to size, so that the strongest words I could muster were, "No problem."

During each session, I lay on my back on the couch. She sat just behind my head. The room lights were dimmed. After a moment of quiet, she began the induction, speaking slowly and softly, with long pauses between each gentle suggestion. Her seductive, mesmerizing voice seemed to be coming from my head, as if I were listening to a stereo recording through earphones.

"Let's begin by taking a deep breath and exhaling slowly through the nose. Feel the tension leaking from your body. Again, draw a deep breath, and this time envision it seeping out each and every pore of your skin, cleansing, relaxing, like a warm bath. Once more. Breathe deeply and think of yourself as a helium-filled balloon, at first straining its cord, then gradually losing lift as the gas escapes, until you shrink and sink softly to the ground.

"Notice the waves of contentment surging up your spine, each stronger than the last. Follow them as they fan out to soothe your neck muscles. Feel their warmth overspread your scalp from back to front. See how they feather out and lift off your forehead to rejoin and augment the next wave, building a cumulus cloud of peace around you, insulating, cushioning.

"Now your guide's healing fingers are beginning to massage your forehead, smoothing the wrinkles as they spread to your temples, where they draw little curlicues that spiral outward, passing just behind each ear. Now the hands of your guide come gently to rest beside your head.

"Envision yourself sitting on your sumptuous cloud. You become aware of a friendly number five, fluffy soft and powder blue, standing on the edge of your cloud, facing you. He's smiling and bearing gifts for you. You smile back. He strolls toward you and places the gifts at your feet. You deserve them. They're his way of thanking you for being who you are, unique, special. Having performed his mission, he drifts off and evaporates.

"You notice a warm zephyr brush your right cheek and turn to see a slender and lovely, pink number four approaching. She brings you the four winds: north, east, south and west, representing the four elements: earth, wind, fire and water. Each in turn breathes its characteristic temperature and humidity on a part of your body needing to feel it. The dry north wind cools your brow. The raw east wind moistens your lips with brine. The sultry south wind whispers passion in your ear. And the crisp west wind tingles your nose, refreshing every breath you draw, filling you with energy. When the winds have spoken, she curtsies and takes her leave.

"Do you hear that tinkle of laughter on your left? The infectious giggle of a contented baby? Look down beside you. It's a cherubic, inflated, yellow number three, and he's dying to exhale his joyous vapors around you. All he needs is your smile of permission. There. He's deflating. Feel each bubble of joy he exhales for you, tickle your skin. Your whole body feels alive, sensitive, receptive. He's getting very small now. Thank him before he disappears.

"Energized, you stand and stretch. Take a few steps. Notice how springy the cloud feels under your feet. Look up. Who's that gliding toward you? Why, it's a slinky, warm, red number two. She alights before you. Reach out and stroke her curves. Smooth. If you slide your hand down her back, she'll glide to one side, like an automatic sliding door, revealing a secret passageway beyond. See? The way is illuminated by a brilliant white light. You walk toward its source and find that it radiates from a pristine, handsome number one. He ushers you through a door at the end of the corridor. And who do you think that number one is, Karcher? It's you. You are number one. Karcher is number one.

"You enter a quiet room. It's your special room, laid out and decorated just the way you designed it. Take a moment to look around and get comfortable.

"You're safe here. You can be alone, undisturbed. No one can enter without your permission."

I envisioned a small gymnasium with windows high on the west wall, too high for anyone outside to see me. Shafts of sunlight beamed to the polished maple floor. There was only one door, just big enough for a person to enter. It was double bolted and kept locked at all times. A couch along the east side was the only furniture in my room. I sat on the couch, and sometimes, in later sessions, I admitted my guide to sit with me and discuss things. But for now it was enough just to have my sanctum.

After I'd spent several minutes in silence, looking around my room, Dr. Locke would remind me that I could return whenever I pleased, that there I would never be disturbed. In my room, she said, I was number one, the boss, always in control. Then she would gently awaken me on a slow count to five. We'd discuss in hushed tones in the dark my residual, warm feelings of power. During these early sessions, I gained sufficient strength to trust that my feelings were valid, acceptable, even good. I came away increasingly puffed up with a sense of who I was. It could almost be called pride.

Dr. Locke was fast becoming my savior, her weekly infusions of self-worth convincing to the point of addiction. But the breadth of my addiction — carefully orchestrated, I later learned — was yet to surface.

The hook was set slowly, without so much as a wince from the patient. I was having so much fun getting high on myself that I was totally unaware of the operation. I anesthetized myself with endorphins at the mere sound of her voice. Thus insulated from pain, I could safely take control. Or so it seemed. And that was the deadly deceit, for it was Auburn Locke and not I who took control of Karcher.

Chapter 6

PATTIN

Whoever was in control, it felt wonderful, and I took my joy home to Witte. As long as I could look forward to my fix on Wednesdays, I could face anything, even Witte's abrupt announcement to her parents at Thanksgiving dinner: "Karcher and I are going to have a baby."

Before I could say, "We are?" Loring quipped, "Young lady, *you* may be going to have a baby; *he* has nothing more to do with it."

Witte had wisely waited until her father had finished his goose to divulge the confidence. But poor Ida, a slow eater, began to choke on her mouthful of stuffing and received a resounding clap on the back from Loring before I, sitting closest to her, could respond. To my relief, the focus shifted for several seconds to the usually unobtrusive little woman at my left, hacking and spewing bread crumbs.

"My Lord," Ida gasped at last, then nearly disappeared into the calico quilting of her chair. I couldn't tell, especially not from the side view of her expression, whether she was experiencing pain or pleasure; even her full visage was difficult to read, so deeply buried were her feelings. Her mask was Tragedy wizened, a compressed loss, indelibly written.

Loring, as always, got straight to the point. "You're not built for whelping, Witte." Judging by the rapidity of his head rocking and the intensity of his masticating, which in the absence of food and teeth produced indelicate smacking and clicking, I deduced that Loring was more upset about Witte's condition than Ida or I.

"Just because I have a narrow waist, don't mean I'm close built." Witte illustrated her assertion by standing and slapping her hips.

Undaunted, Loring continued. "You'll need Doc Morton to pull you through. Most a them fellas up to Maine Medical never seen a filly like you. They're used to the rugged ones that drop 'em easy."

Ida sat up suddenly. "Why, for heaven's sake, Loring. She's a woman, not a bisque doll. They'll *take* the baby if they have to."

It was the mechanics of birthing, not the pregnancy or its timing, that concerned Witte's parents. The shock of the announcement damped out quickly inside their resilient and practical skulls, and they turned their attention to preparation for the inevitable.

I, on the other hand, was feeling worse by the second, like a carp suffocating in an undersized aquarium, and excused myself to gulp air outside the kitchen door. Grotesque images flashed upon my mind's flickering screen, framed rapidly and subliminally at first, then gradually slower and longer in duration as my hyperventilation supplied excess oxygen, until I was able to view them individually: Witte, her abdomen inflated like Tweedle Dum, her tiny head listing to starboard and bobbing, her long arms gyrating pointlessly, wobbling toward me on the Old Orchard pier, singing a fractured rendition of "We Must Be Vigilant" ("American Patrol" plagiarized for dancing); Loring, three times his normal size, towering over me, grinning like an imbecile; illuminated tenement windows freeze-framed in random order, revealing a domestic quarrel, a burglar in full cry, lovers hard at work, a man brushing his teeth, and a Saint Bernard puppy defecating on a white rug. I'd just focused on a portrait of Nettie in our living room, her right hand raised with the Hoffritz aimed at her heart, when the door opened behind me, shorting the sinister projector inside my head.

I turned to see Witte, smiling cautiously from the opening a step above me. Drawn ever so slightly taut, her full lower lip became almost a mirror image of the one above. "You okay, dear?"

"Uh, sure. Just getting a breath of air. I always eat too much on Thanksgiving."

"It's going to be all right, Karcher." For a moment, Witte stood, smoothing the knife pleats of her Black Watch plaid wool skirt across her belly. Then, unable to contain her joy, she twirled out the door and jumped into my arms.

I staggered, caught my balance and waited for her hair to settle, then pumped my arms a little, trying to detect any change in her mass. I could swear she weighed more than when I carried her, giddy and kicking, to the bed the night before.

"Are you sure, Witte?"

"Sure I'm broad enough?" She draped an arm around my neck, pulled herself up, nipped my ear and whispered: "'Course I am, silly."

"No, damn it, sure that you're pregnant?"

Witte snap-arched her back, forcing me to put her down. She spun to face me, but I eluded her scrutiny by looking over her shoulder at Loring's D6 Caterpillar dozer cozying up to a pile of manure back of the barn.

"A woman knows."

Witte's answer, breathed deep and slow, carried such authority that I dared not pursue the matter further.

She sighed full in my face, slid past me and let herself back inside. I remained on the stoop, inhaling her scent, which hung in the still air, persistent, pungent and irresistibly earthy. Then, following its trail, I found myself beside her at the sink with a dish towel in my hand. She was mixing the dishwater, simultaneously pouring from the steaming kettle while stroking the Myers pump. I gently praised her coordination, but she ignored me. When she turned to replace the kettle on the wood range, I noticed that her eyes avoided mine. Her mouth was small and set.

Quietly, so as not to arouse Ida, who was busy scraping the leftovers from pots at the sideboard, I leaned toward Witte's left ear and asked: "Have you been to the doctor?"

Her hands never faltered in the suds, and the dishes began to overcrowd the rack, which I had been inattentive at emptying. I barely heard her delayed answer, "No," directed at the splash board.

"Then you don't really know," I replied more forcefully.

"I know."

"How?" I said, loud enough for Ida to hear. Witte returned the pot in her hand to the rinse water, dried her hands and faced me.

"Lost my breakfast yesterday, if you must know. And I missed this month." She frowned. "I'm not sick, either."

"No, I should say you're not," Ida added from the pantry.

I had to agree. Witte looked positively radiant, especially so when angry. The way her chest heaved with the force of each breath made me want to drag her behind the guest room door. There was no question in my mind that I could still encircle her waist with my hands. She couldn't be pregnant.

During my brief fantasy, Witte had returned to the sink with the kettle and was warming the rinse water. "Rack's full, Karcher. Get on with it."

She refilled the kettle with vigorous swipes at the pump handle, pausing at the bottom of each stroke to allow the foot valve to seat, which set off a procession of water hammers that rang from the galvanized suction line — "clank, clank, clank" — then returned the kettle to the front burner and spun open the draft.

"I think she means it, Karcher," Ida said, raising her right eyebrow as she passed me. "Might's well get used to it."

* * * * * * * *

Doc Morton was consulted on Monday and later confirmed what Witte already knew. I took to rising early, munching a stale doughnut and dashing from the apartment before Witte woke up and got sick, which she did earlier and more frequently in the days that followed. Having accidentally swallowed an eye screw at age five and been forced by my father the anatomist to drink a saturated saline solution until I disgorged the entire contents of my stomach into the bathtub, where he searched in vain for the thing on hands and knees, I felt more than revulsion at being confined with anyone feeling nauseous, even if for a good cause. My terror stemmed from the unshakable belief that I would catch the "bug" and follow suit. The fact that my companion was not contagious held no sway. I invariably panicked and fled.

Ironically, I was seldom systemically sick to my stomach, even as a child. After puberty, I only regurgitated as a result of my anxieties, one of which was self-fulfilling. Virus epidemics passed me by, leaving at most a gurgle in my intestines. Perhaps it was my cast iron constitution that kept food flowing mostly in the right direction. At least, that was Witte's theory.

Weekends were the most difficult; I didn't have to leave for work and tended to oversleep. All too often, my alarm was the sound of Witte retching at close range. When I was lucky enough to awaken before she did, if I was feeling especially brave, I'd make her a piece of dry toast and leave it on the bedside table before bolting for the door. After walking the wharves for an hour or so, I'd sneak back to check the status of the curtains in the bedroom. If they were open, I'd check the kitchen for signs of life. Usually, I'd see her through the window, hair pulled back, face drawn, padding about in my old flannel shirt, fixing breakfast, and know that it was safe to return.

She'd insist on frying me eggs and bacon and building a brace of blueberry muffins from scratch, which she knew to be a favorite of mine. But it was impossible to enjoy them while watching her peaked face across the table studying mine while she sipped plain yogurt resembling Phillips Milk of Magnesia from an egg-tarnished silver spoon.

Invariably, by eleven the ordeal was over. She would be dressed, perky and ravenously hungry, and I could relax. It was a complete transformation, and every bit as confusing as Nettie's recovery from a binge. But unlike my alcoholic mother, Witte could recall her recent past; she simply chose not to focus on it.

"Karcher," she announced one bright Sunday noon in January, with half a sandwich stuffed into her cheek, "let's go sledding up to Libby's."

"Do you think that's wise in your condition?"

"My condition, sir, is tops," which she demonstrated convincingly by jumping up from the table and twirling three times in front of me. "See?"

I wanted to ask, "How can you spin like that after this morning?" but the glow on her cheeks and her impish smile told me to shut up. Witte wanted to play, and I needed the exercise.

* * * * * * * *

With spring came a reprieve from the morning sickness and a change in Witte's center of gravity. She had become bow-heavy, a comically grotesque distortion which widened her track and slowed her gait from its usual lunge and sway to a waddle. I felt sorry for her. But more than sympathy—or fear, as the threat of her infecting me with gastric disorder subsided—I felt anger building. This creature growing inside her was diverting her attention from my needs. Her appetite for sex, usually insatiable, diminished to disinterest. And, for the first time in our relationship, Witte was becoming dependent on me.

"Karcher, dear," she would call sweetly from the sofa, "would you bring me my mendin'; it's over there by the phone."

I'd hang about, pacing, hoping that she'd need me for something critical, like taking her to the hospital, but we had several more months of ballooning to endure. She'd summon me often to share her delight at feeling new life stirring inside her. "Come quick, dear." I'd rush to her side, sure that she was about to give birth. She'd take my hand and place it on her belly. "Can you feel her kicking?"

Witte always addressed our fetus as feminine, and, hearing the echo of her words on Thanksgiving—"A woman knows"—I never questioned her source.

* * * * * * * *

It was more than mere coincidence that Witte's reduced sexual appetite and increasing dependency coincided with a shift in my feelings for Auburn Locke.

Well before my mother's suicide, when she had begun to lose control of herself and her family, I began an all-consuming search for her replacement. I needed a woman who could supply order and meaning to life without Nettie. Witte had done all that and more. But now, with our child growing inside her and consuming her attention, she could no longer be counted on to meet my needs, and my latent fear of abandonment resurfaced.

Since I was already in therapy for anxiety, it was natural that I share my orphan phobia with Dr. Locke. Her treatment involved more ego-building hypnosis sessions which had evolved into forty-minute flights of fantasy in which she assisted my passage to my "room" and then turned me loose to explore relationships with others, especially with my mother, in the safety of my sanctum. There I could say things to Nettie I had been unable to vocalize in life, for fear of an irrational response. In my room, my mother, sitting across from me on the couch I provided for our discussions, and coached by Auburn's soothing voice, responded to my questions compassionately. She became an equal instead of a tyrant. As Nettie's love for me became apparent, I began to sob. Afterwards, I'd receive encouragement and a fragrant tissue from the doctor, and left these sessions feeling as if I'd been inflated with helium.

In May, while under Dr. Locke's spell during an especially emotional confrontation with Nettie, I became so distracted by the feelings welling inside me that I blurted: "I think I'm falling in love with you, Auburn."

Close beside my right ear I heard an extra earthy whisper. "That's perfectly natural, Karcher. Go on."

"No, it's crazy," I replied, eyes still closed but suddenly acutely aware of my surroundings: the sound and scent of

Auburn's breathing, the whoosh of an occasional car passing, the crackle from the plugged precipitator in the waiting room, the whir of the tape recorder behind me. (I had given Dr. Locke permission to record each session for her research library.) "I'm married to a wonderful woman who is soon to have our child."

"You're just beginning to experience transference, Karcher. That's a fancy word for what happens when a patient becomes attached to his physician. It happens often in therapy, and we can deal with it."

"I feel so grateful to you for showing me how to love myself, that I love you. Just the sound of your voice makes me swoon. I can't explain it."

"You've explained it very well. I care a lot about you, too, Karcher. Now, I'm afraid it's time to stop. I'm very proud of the progress you're making. Next week we'll try something different: face-to-face therapy instead of hypnosis."

Gently, she elevated my knees and extracted the blanket roll she always placed there for leg support while I was under. Her touch felt different this time, strangely stimulating, like the tingle from an electrical ground fault. I could swear I saw more than compassion in her eyes when she said good night at the door. But she was a doctor and used to such attachments.

* * * * * * * *

Arriving home frustrated and confused, when I caught sight of Witte-the-Great framed in the kitchen window, towel-wrapped, fresh from the shower, raking her tresses over the radiator, I felt sick with guilt. I didn't dare tell her what had happened, and I couldn't stomach the thought of not telling her. She had always been die straight with me, even when what she had to say was unpleasant. I respected that, especially so after having suffered Nettie's duplicity. But this feeling for Auburn had caught me off guard.

No problem, I reassured myself. I'm under orders not to discuss what goes on in therapy, but to review each session in solitude, where it will do the most good. With my secret sanctioned, I felt secure in confronting Witte, and seized the door handle. It was locked.

Of course it was locked; it was nine at night in Portland and Witte was alone. So why did it seem unusual? I reached for my key and was in the process of inserting it when the door was opened from inside.

"Huy, big fella."

With my head down, I plunged into Witte's waiting arms, buried my face in the billow of damp silk that fell across her neck and shoulder, and hung on.

"Rough one this week?"

"Uh-huh."

Witte allowed me to hold her in the doorway for over a minute until I could pull myself away. When I did, I tried to avoid her eyes searching mine, to not notice her lower lip tucked under her incisors or the furrows between her impossibly raked eyebrows. But it was no use. She held her ground and my gaze, breathing deeply for the three of us as she mirrored my expression of torment.

I tried to back towards the door to escape, but my feet wouldn't move. I opened my mouth to speak, but no words came out. I was trapped between guilt and passion, incapacitated by indecision. Deceit was not in my repertoire; I had to force myself to sustain it, and it showed.

"She got a hold on you, Karcher?" Witte's head was now tipped, and her eyes had hardened.

"Don't be ridiculous," I said too quickly. "She's just reopening old wounds to bathe them in the light of logic, so they'll heal. I've got to go through this to get better."

"I see." Witte smoothed her hair, turned and waddled into the kitchen, calling over her shoulder. "Cup of chamomile'll settle your system. I could use some myself."

"I'm fine." My feeble protest sounded even less convincing than my alibi, and Witte simply ignored it.

* * * * * * *

By late June the sun was strong enough to burn the frequent fogs that blanketed the waterfront. Windows opened along Pine Street. Children's laughter could be heard outdoors for the first time since Halloween. Inside 157B, there was more going on than the usual spring cleaning.

Our bed had been displaced to make room for the cradle-boat, a miniature peapod that Loring had fashioned from old rain barrel staves and suspended with cod line from a crude oak frame. In it was a muslin pillow embroidered with pink impatiens blossoms and a tiny matching pink crocheted blanket, both Ida's handiwork. The gender of our child had never been in question in the Murch family.

My desk in the corner had been swept clean of its dusty piles of model airplane magazines and marine engine brochures, thoroughly scrubbed and redecorated with all the trappings of an efficient baby service center. Even the drawers had been turned out and refilled with diapers, pins, receiving blankets, towels, cotton balls and baby oil. In the bottom right drawer was an assortment of hand-me-down sun suits, pinafores, buntings, and mittens even smaller than Witte's. The bathroom, too, showed signs of anticipation: the new Rubbermaid tub—in pink, of course—next to the sink, with a chartreuse canister of Phisohex beside it. On the bedside table lay an already dog-eared paperback of Dr. Spock. Even our gauze bedroom curtains, fresh from the laundry, fluttered expectantly.

We didn't have to wait much longer. True to form, Witte went into labor precisely nine months to the day she figured she'd been impregnated, on October the ninth, 1960. I was in the throes of a recurring nightmare about four in the morning when she woke me with an agonizing groan.

It was August, 1939, and Witte and I were teenagers, walking the Boston & Maine track in a narrow cut just outside Pine Point, when my acute hearing discriminated from a background twitter of finches the faint bark of a steam locomotive crossing the Fore River bridge, accelerating south. I figured we had less than five minutes to clear the mile long cut before being sucked under its churning drivers, and towed Witte to a run between the rails. We were making good speed, timing our leaps to the rhythm of the ties, and would have easily made it to the south exit before the commuter train took us, when Witte tripped and fell, twisting her ankle in the process. As I bent to her aid, the sun was put out behind us. I glanced over my shoulder to see Number 3663's dusky mask entering the cut, chime whistle in full cry, stack pouring a pall of doom. I reached to lift her, but my two year old arms were too short. My stubby fingers fanned in vain toward her. I tried to scream but could only squeak. Over the ominous thunder of the inexorably advancing Pacific, I barely heard Witte's cry.

"Call Doc Morton."

"Oh, God, no," I moaned, coming to.

"Pattin's comin', Karcher."

"Who?" I said, now fully awake and sitting up, wiping the sweat from my brow. I snapped on the light.

"Our little girl, dear. Go call Doc, quick. I'm havin' contractions."

"Sorry, I was in the middle of a bad dream. What did you say her name was?"

"Pattin—P-A-T-T-I-N—Like the general, only feminine."

"That's the name of an oil field engine, Witte."

"Yes, I know. That's why I thought you'd like it. Besides, aren't all engines addressed as 'she'?" Witte winced and panted until the next cramp passed. "*Now*, Karcher. Quick."

"What if she's a boy?" I knew the answer before I asked.

"A woman knows these things. Now, please hurry."

After making the call and grabbing Witte's toilet articles, I eased my puffing primipara into the A for the short trip up the hill. We met Doc Morton at Maine Medical at the hour of the wolf. He was most cordial, considering the time I'd awakened him, and let me accompany Witte into the labor room.

Doc asked me to step into the hall while he examined her. Through the open door I heard his jovial bass. "Let's have a look, Doll. Boy, you weren't kidding. Another hour should do it."

As he beckoned me to return, I heard a thick little voice over his shoulder: "It's a girl, Doc."

"That so?" Doc raised an eyebrow in my direction.

I was allowed to stay with Witte until they wheeled her to the delivery room. We set up a routine to ease the pain. They had music in the labor room, Latin dance music, mostly rumbas and sambas. When she felt a contraction coming, Witte would get onto all fours, and I'd begin pummeling her back in time to the music, trying to match the intensity of my blows with her efforts, taking my cue from her breathing. The door was open, and after we were at it awhile, a nurse's aide poked her head in. She ducked out quickly and began whispering anxiously to someone in the hall.

"There's a man in there, and he's pounding on her backside."

I recognized Doc's voice. "Never mind. Whatever they're doing is fine. She hasn't asked for any medication."

A moment later Doc popped in, wearing a broad smile. "Hate to break up a good team at work, but I must check the patient's progress. Karcher, once more, if you don't mind."

While I waited in the hall, I could hear Doc relaxing Witte with his wit. "Warms my heart to see a couple still cooperating at this stage. Usually, the missus is yelling obscenities at her husband by now, whether he's present or not." He paused. "And you, young lady, are about to deliver. Nurse."

I took my cue, returning just to kiss Witte's damp forehead, then let myself out.

The waiting room was deserted, which was both a relief and a disappointment; I didn't want to reveal my anxiety but desperately wanted to share my excitement, as if alone in the still of a moonlit field I had unearthed the rusty hulk of another one-lunger that I had to have but couldn't tell Nettie about. My only potential audience was the receptionist behind glass, but she looked morose and unapproachable, so I took a seat in the far corner and sought solace from Ann Landers. Quickly exhausting her advice, I tried to take a coffee break, but the dispenser in the hall had ingested a slug and refused the real thing. Back on my feet with nowhere to go, I began pacing.

For the first time I allowed myself to question how it all happened. It certainly hadn't been planned, my timely deployment of XXXX protection having been rigidly followed. Then I vaguely recalled the evening that Witte milked me to sleep. Perhaps there had been another seduction with penetration while I was semiconscious. She was such a needy rascal—then. And I could sleep through almost anything. I tried in vain to remember having a wet dream in early October and felt my ears burn with humiliation. What a chump, to be caught off guard.

But I couldn't blame her. My depressions had left little appetite for sex, and Witte, resourceful as ever, had made the best of it. There was no malice to it; it wasn't in her. Witte always played by the rules of her heart. Lust and love conspired to rouse her in the night, and I, as always, responded to her touch.

As I was chastising myself mid pace for questioning Witte's motives, the waiting room doors swung wide, and Doc Morton approached, rubbing his hands. "Your Witte's quite the psychic, Karcher. She just gave you a loud little girl—eight pounds, three ounces—full term and awful feisty. Keep you two busy." He extended a large, warm hand in my direction. "Needed some assisting, but I didn't have to do a C-section. Baby's head'll look funny for a while, from the forceps." I felt the blood draining from my brain. "Don't worry, she'll fill right out in a day or two."

When I'd extricated my stomach from my throat and could breathe again, I asked if I could see them. "Sure," boomed Doc, "but Witte's bit groggy. They're in room thirty-seven."

I met the same incredulous nurse's aide in the hall. She recognized me immediately and escorted me with mute excitement to Witte's room. The door was ajar, but I knocked softly before entering. I wasn't ready for the scene. Witte's color was barely warmer than the pillow, and her hair streamed without direction like the feathers of a road-pressed raven. Tucked in beside her, crimson and quivering with rage, was an apple doll whose crushed forehead receded like the blade of a shovel. It, too, had a copious crop of black hair, splashed in damp disarray across her mother's arm.

Witte licked her lips and struggled to greet me. "Sorry she's so noisy, dear." (I hadn't noticed the insistent saw-whet scraping noise at her elbow.)

"She's so…so tiny."

"Yes, but she compensates with her lungs, and they're almost as big as mine."

"Not quite," I said, feeling much relieved that Witte's sense of humor hadn't gone the way of her color. Gingerly, I took a seat on the edge of the bed opposite the shriveled product of our mysterious union. "And how are you doing, brave girl?"

"Good enough, I guess," she replied with a stoic Murch jut of the chin. "Doc says this stuff'll wear off in an hour or two. Didn't want to take it, Karcher, but Doc, he insisted."

Feeling a little faint, I quickly changed the subject. "Kid's hungry as hell, by the sound of her. Are you breast feeding?"

"Well, I sure don't intend on bursting." Witte drew the sheet down just enough to reveal her engorged condition.

"Jeezus," I gasped involuntarily. "You better get to it."

"And I think it's time your wife got some rest, Mr. Stickney." I turned to see a barrel-chested white uniform standing over me. Judging from this nurse's size and the set of her jaw, I deduced that I'd been given an order, and snapped to my feet.

Before I was out of reach, Witte stretched a pale but shapely arm and brushed my cheek with her hand. "We'll be fine, dear." She looked down at our daughter, who had for the moment stopped crying, and added, "She won't be no trouble."

Chapter 7

SEDUCTION

No doubt Witte's pregnancy had accelerated my headlong plunge into the web of Auburn Locke. But what started as an innocent and manageable transference the previous fall, had snowballed into a full-fledged infatuation by April, thanks in no small part to the deceit of my doctor, whose overtures were so skillfully crafted that I was unaware of losing control until it was too late.

Auburn's insidious plot, I learned much later, was to add me to her list of lovers. One by one, she duped each member of her revolving club of suitors into believing he was the only man in her life. It always started, as mine had, with individual therapy, where she could judge the receptiveness of her prey and work the best approach for his seduction. As a hypnotherapist—and a consummate one, I might add—Locke had the ideal tool for softening her patient's defenses before injecting her venom. Once her male prospect declared his love for her, which took anywhere from five hypnosis sessions for the most vulnerable to no more than twenty for the hardest catch, she'd switch to eye contact.

We'd sit face to face in opposing chairs in her dimly lit "closing" room. If there had been any doubt about my feelings for Auburn while under the spell of her voice alone, lying on her couch in the dark, they were undeniable now. Her green eyes, dilated and shaded by the shadows, burning into mine, buried her barb deep in my heart.

These sessions had all the trappings of conventional psychotherapy: the patient, encouraged to free associate with gentle prodding from the analyst, spilling his guts; the doctor, largely silent, listening, occasionally asking questions or making observations. To an untrained observer, the procedure would appear strictly professional. But to her quarry, Auburn's egotistical ministry was as stealthily invasive as cancer.

Mostly it was Auburn's body that conveyed her message: The way she smoothed her hose after crossing her legs, from the ankle up, slowly, with the toe of her shoe pointed in my direction. The way she placed her hands on the arms of her chair, her wrists elevated, her fingers barely touching the upholstery. Try as I might to stay on the topic of the hour, even one as crucial to my sanity as fear of abandonment, my mind would return again and again to the only subject that really mattered: our relationship.

By mid May, I was beside myself with curiosity. "Doctor, I have to ask. Do you feel the same way about me that I do about you?"

"And what exactly is that, Karcher?"

"You know."

"Why don't you tell me again."

"My insides are turning handsprings for you. I want to hold you so bad, I ache."

For the first time during a session, Auburn rose from her chair and approached me. Only once, when a tremor took her by surprise, did her eyes leave mine as she moved to sit at my feet and arrange her skirt in a fan across her lap. When she'd composed herself, she answered me in deep, dulcet tones.

"I'm very flattered, Karcher. Women my size don't hear that very often." She raised a very warm, fleshy hand to my cheek and held it there. I felt like I was going to pass out.

Sitting below me, gazing up into my eyes, Auburn appeared doting as a teenage date—"sickly sweet," as Nettie would say. The top of her head was surprisingly slender, inviting me to place my hand there and stroke her hair. After I'd run my fingers slowly a second time through her auburn locks, she took my hand and kissed it dead center on the palm. Then she breathed the longest sigh I'd ever heard and ended it with a smile.

"Let's move to the couch, Karcher, where we can be more comfortable."

We did, and immediately became entwined. Auburn soon gravitated to a horizontal position, lying across my lap, her eyes continuing to search mine for sustenance. I cradled her head in my arms and gushed like a moonstruck adolescent.

"I just love to hear you talk," she confessed when I'd run out of adjectives. "You express yourself so beautifully, I could listen to you for hours."She paused, dropped her gaze and took my left hand in hers. "And—this is going to sound silly—you have the most beautiful hands. They're so strong, and yet they look gentle as a baby's." She worked her fingers through mine and gave my wedding ring a little twist. "See how your fingers taper? That's unusual in a man." She looked up again. "I think that's what attracts me so to you: your gentle appearance and deceptive strength, not to mention your eyes."

I crushed her in my embrace and marveled at her heft as I rocked her in my arms. "You know the reason I love you? I just figured it out. You're so substantial."

"Substantial? Well, sir, I've never been called *that* before." Her wink erased my uneasiness before it got a grip.

"I've only held a woman like you once before, when I was sixteen. Her name was Melissa Easthope. We met on the dance floor at Perkins's Pavilion in Naples. Mel picked me out of the crowd, dragged me onto the floor and gave me a bear hug I'll never forget. We danced a few slow numbers then went skinny dipping in the brook back of the barn."

Auburn raised a throaty chuckle, sat up and kissed me on the cheek. "Karcher, this has been heavenly, but I'm afraid our time is up."

It was as if she'd pulled my main fuse. "No. Please. We can't stop like that. I mean, it's artificial to limit our time together to fifty minutes, now that we... Listen, I...I can't be your patient anymore. I love you, and I think you love me, too. To call our relationship therapy is dishonest. Can't we see each other more often? Can't I stay longer? Of course, I'll continue to pay you, but I can't treat you as my doctor."

"I think it's wise we keep this apparently professional, Karcher. Remember, I have other patients. Besides, I don't think your wife would take kindly to my extending the length of your appointments." She smiled. "Think of yourself as my client and secret admirer."

"Auburn, I...I don't think I can last the week without seeing you again. Can't we meet, say, for lunch sometime, before the next session?"

"That wouldn't be a good idea just now, Karcher. I think we should keep our relationship in this room, don't you?"

"Oh, yes. Yes, of course."

Auburn rose to her feet. "You *have* come a long way, Karcher." I stood. "Just look at you," she continued, "a monarch in charge of his fate. Congratulations, sir."

She escorted me to the door, wrapped her arms around my neck and drew me to her. We kissed, this time on the lips. I could feel it was mutual. As I pulled away, she draped herself on the door and blew me another kiss. Reluctantly, I let myself out.

As my body was anesthetized, my soul led me home that night.

* * * * * * * *

It was essential that I suppress my ecstasy in Witte's presence—not a difficult task, I thought, considering how ingrained was my misery. My concern for Witte-the-Great and our child in utero made it easier for me to ignore my role as lover, and play expectant father, which required frequent frowning. But when we went grocery shopping Saturday morning, the cart, whose frame was bent so that one wheel remained slightly elevated, began to jiggle at idle, accompanied by muffled putts from its one-cylinder "engine," while it waited for Witte to select and load a can of soup. When she moved on to the next aisle, the cart would shudder and emit heavier thuds as it accelerated in pursuit.

"Karcher, that you chuffin'?"

The engine immediately fell silent, and Witte, absorbed with shopping, didn't pursue the matter.

But later, at the checkout line, the impatient cart resumed rocking, shuddering at each reversal when the engine fired. Witte reached to offload a jiggling grapefruit, stopped herself and turned to study my face.

"I'm not crazy. It *is* you."

The engine stalled without so much as a hiccup. (Very unrealistic, I thought.)

"What?"

"You know perfectly well, Karcher."

"What on earth are you talking about?"

"Just help me with this stuff. We'll discuss it later."

Not a single chuff of ecstasy escaped Witte's acute antennae. I would have to explain myself. Maybe she'd accept it if I characterized the phenomenon as a recurrence of my childhood practice of imitating one-lungers whenever I was bored; it was mostly the truth. I wrestled the grocery bags into the Model A, settled behind the wheel and waited.

"Karcher, the ice cream's meltin'."

"Didn't you want to ask me about something?"

"Not now, dear." She reached for the key and popped out the ignition cylinder.

Witte had a habit of stockpiling data on a subject until her brain became so full of it she'd have to unload. This she did in one horrendous eruption, the verbal equivalent to my boyhood bathtub scene. Invariably of late, the subject was me, and the data wasn't complimentary. I never knew when she was going to dump. Something I said or did, however innocuous at the time, would open her flood gates and the invectives would flow. Once she started, there was no stopping her until the last infraction had been disgorged. I sensed that the shopping cart incident was pushing her storage to near capacity, which meant that on this subject a lot more had been recorded than I had dreamed possible.

But guilt and the sensitivity of the matter had conspired to alert me to the proximity of a drubbing, and I was more prepared than usual. Ironically, it was one of my attempts to compensate her for my inattention that set her spilling over.

It was an unusually balmy Sunday in early June, about a month before Pattin hatched. Witte was up on a stool in bare feet at the open bedroom window, starting to hang the curtains, when I entered the room. I made a dash to her side and called her down on account of safety, offering to take over. As I did so, I seized her arm to steady her descent.

That was a mistake.

One thing you didn't do with Witte was restrain her by force. However risky, it was better to let her complete the task she'd selected for herself without assistance. Headstrong was putting it mildly.

"Now, look," (I knew I was in for it whenever I heard those words, but I was never sure how much more was coming.) "I've had about enough of your help. I may be off

balance as a Maytag, but I know my limitations. Grabbin'
me like that'll tip me over for sure."

"Okay, okay, but I worry about..."

"Don't interrupt me." She put down the curtain and
moved to face me eyeball to eyeball, so close that her
distended belly brushed my groin.

"You've been actin' awful queer these last few weeks:
Interferin' with my preparations for the baby; so overeager
to help me in the kitchen; buzzin' carousel tunes in the
shower; barkin' like a one-lunger when we go for a walk—
and in the supermarket, f'god's sake."

"I'm just excited about having a kid, I guess."

"Horsefeathers. You're scared of the human body."

"Not of yours." I reached to embrace her, but my wrists
were gripped and I was shoved backward.

"You don't fool me one bit, Karcher. There's somethin'
else goin' on."

"Believe me or not; I don't care. This baby has got me
turned inside out. Sure, I'm scared. Of it, and of you,
carrying it, but it's exciting, too. Gives me a feeling of pride
to sire a child."

Witte's eyes softened a little but did not leave mine. "I
just can't figure you out. One minute you're terrified my
being pregnant's going to make you sick. Next minute
you're carryin' on like a rooster. Maybe Dr. Locke can make
sense of it."

I swallowed hard. "Th...that's a good idea, Witte. I'll
bring it up at our next session."

Chapter 8

HEARTWORM

Under the care of Dr. Locke my open heart became infected as an innocent and trusting spaniel's heart becomes infested with worms, insidiously. With my defenses down, Auburn's "filaria" took possession of not only my heart but my mind. Symptoms began to appear in midsummer, the worst of which was a change in the color of my thinking.

At some point shortly after she decided to love me, Auburn became jealous of Witte. (Auburn couldn't be accused of falling in love; with her it was a calculated move.) As with her plot to entrap me, I learned this much later. At the time I just felt resentment building against Witte.

When I described Witte's latest diatribe, Auburn dismissed it as a normal prenatal syndrome. "Most expectant mothers get edgy in the third trimester, Karcher. She'll come around once the baby's born."

Then the subtle subterfuge. "Witte sounds like a fine, strong woman, but I'm concerned about the control she has over you. That could undermine the sense of self you've developed. Remember: Karcher is in control. Karcher is king of Karcher."

I felt my king diminish to a little prince in the presence of queen mother Locke, who knew just how to manipulate my size to ensure that I never grew more powerful than she. For it was Auburn and not Witte who controlled me.

Auburn wasn't bashful about not playing by the rules of her profession, freely admitting that her approach was 'unconventional, tailored to suit the needs of each client.' In fact, her methods were adjusted to infiltrate the hearts of her patients according to their receptivity. So cunning was her craft, that she seldom failed to ensnare her victims, so long as she met with them individually. But her insatiable ego needed grander proof of her prowess, and she decided to group her favorites to bask in love augmented. It ultimately proved her undoing.

Even a consummate actress would founder attempting to play several roles at the same time, but Auburn assigned herself the impossible task of rotating half a dozen roles in the space of five minutes during a fan club picnic she devised.

At the conclusion of our session she announced her scheme. "I'm having a summer solstice picnic at Deering Oaks next Sunday for my patients and their spouses. Very informal. Everyone is to bring their own munchies. I'm providing the patties, dogs, ice and drinks: soda, iced tea and lemonade—no liquor, Karcher. We'll fire up the grills about five o'clock. It'll be a chance to meet others on your wavelength. I hope you and Witte can come."

"I don't know. Witte's getting close to the wire and doesn't move far from a phone."

"There are phones in the park, Karcher. Besides, the hospital is within spitting distance. You have no excuse."

"What if it rains?"

"The rain date is the following Sunday."

"We'll try, Auburn. You know, if it was just you and I, I'd bring a capon and a dozen roses."

"You're a sweet man, Karcher. Love you."

* * * * * * * *

I arrived home to find Witte scrubbing the bathroom floor on her hands and knees. This time I resisted the temptation to offer assistance and sat on the toilet seat while I relayed Auburn's invitation. Witte loved the outdoors, so I had a fighting chance of convincing her. Using all the arguments in my arsenal, I laid out the contingencies to ease her mind. I even heaped on a little guilt.

"You know how helpful Dr. Locke has been. I think it's the least we can do—that is, if you're up to it. We can play it by ear; she doesn't need an r.s.v.p."

Witte caught the rim of the sink and slowly pulled herself erect. "I don't know. I just don't know. This little girl's wearin' me down." She arched her back and rubbed it over both kidneys. "I'll let you know."

"You're wearing yourself down, Witte. Please let up and give yourself a chance to enjoy life a little."

"Now, don't start. I'll soak in the tub awhile and be fine."

Later, when she'd fallen asleep in my arms as we lay together like nested spoons, I thrilled to the sound of her labored breathing for two. Now and then as I stroked her hair she'd murmur contentedly. During those precious moments before I fell asleep, there was no room for anyone else in my life.

* * * * * * * *

I waited until Sunday morning, when we'd caught up on our sleep, to ask Witte again about the picnic. We were finishing breakfast.

"Looks like a nice day for the picnic."

Witte didn't answer right away. She rose from the table, bused our dishes to the sink and stood at the kitchen window, watching the gulls wheel in and out of the shadows cast by the red brick warehouses, their reflections now and then flashed from the plate glass store fronts across the street. I studied her profile from the table: the power of her omniscient stare, the long straight run of her nose, the stoic set of her lower lip, the thrust of her prominent chin and belly. I felt ashamed, both for being so driven and for what I was putting her through. But I needed her with me to keep my heart in check. And I wanted to show her off to everyone, especially to Auburn. Perhaps I hoped her presence at the picnic would put an end to my agony, that Auburn would be so jealous she'd refuse to see me anymore, or that Witte would deck Auburn for trying to steal me from her.

As so often happened, Witte broke up the fight between my heart and mind. This time she allowed my heart to win. "Could we be back by dark, dear?"

"No problem. It has to be over by dark; there aren't any lights."

"Good, 'cause I gotta get my rest. I'll fix a salad while you get us some buns at Meserve's. Onions, too, Karcher. I'm in the mood for onions. And strawberries."

I was at the door when she called me back. "Haven't you forgotten something?" She toddled to meet me and pressed her great belly against me. I took her in my arms and gently rocked the three of us. She kissed me on the neck, but I couldn't bring myself to reciprocate. When she pulled away, I noticed her eyes were brimming with tears. She said nothing more, but I knew she was already experiencing my distance.

* * * * * * * *

The picnic area was already smudged with an appetizing haze of barbequed burgers and hot dogs when we arrived at a quarter of six. Witte had wisely chosen a pair of moccasins for the quarter mile walk from the parking lot at the far end of the park, but she was puffing like a locomotive by the time we closed on our hostess. Auburn was talking to a burly, bearded man with sandy hair, seated at one of the tables. Three other couples were in a huddle around a smoldering grille. All I could hear of their conversations was coughing as they dodged the fickle smoke.

"Karcher, so glad you could make it." Auburn was dressed in a clinging powder blue shift and smiling expansively.

"Dr. Locke, I'd like you to meet my wife, Witte Murch. As you can see, we're expecting our firstborn soon."

Witte swept her hair from her eyes and leveled their narrow-set, searchlight glare on her opponent. "It's a girl and she's got me awful winded."

"You're a brave woman to join us. I'm honored that you made the effort. Karcher, Witte, this is my husband, Basil."

The large man rose to his full six feet four inches and pressed a mealy hand into mine. As he struggled to speak, his eyelids shut then fluttered ajar and closed again before opening wide. "Glad to meet cha." He blinked rapidly then turned to address Witte, letting his index finger brush her cheek as if he were greeting his favorite granddaughter. "You two are going to have your hands full pretty quick."

Auburn nodded her approval of Witte when only I was looking. "Come, I want you to meet the rest of the gang. This is Harry and his wife, Porcher, from Gorham. And this lanky fella is Fred. Mona, over here, is my backstop; without all her help, this party couldn't have happened. Last, but not least, I want you to meet Doug and his wife, Greer, from Falmouth. Let's see, I think we're all here, and it looks like Mona has the meat waiting for the rolls. Chow down, guys. Drinks and chips are on the table."

Auburn swished away, leaving us to mix for a moment on our own. Thank God for Witte; she plunged right in as if she'd known them all.

"Karcher, here, is from Connecticut, but he's summered up to Sebago ever since he could crawl. I was raised on a farm in Varney. Daddy plays piano in the Grange band. Karcher and I live just over the hill on Pine Street."

After that it was easy. We learned that Harry was a sanitary engineer in charge of Gorham's new waste treatment plant. Neatly groomed with slicked down dark hair and horn rimmed glasses, Harry could pass for any of the white shirts on my floor at Portland Copper. He was a smooth and articulate talker, deadly serious and, as I was to discover, a sneaky devil.

Pudgy Porcher raised malamutes on their eleven-acre tract out on the river road. She worked mostly alone, as Harry was tied to the plant, which needed almost constant attention during its initial phases. Porcher didn't relate well with people; her brusque manner was more suited to her strong-willed brood who responded only to sharp commands and raw meat. Harry was Auburn's patient; Porcher was Auburn's friend.

I could see that Fred was very shy and vulnerable. Single and likely to remain so, he was a challenge to our voracious doctor. In trying to extricate him from his slender chrysalis, Auburn risked destroying him before she could net him. I had the misfortune of watching Fred wither in her grasp. A few months later, sapped of his soul, the poor wretch committed his body to the brine off Portland Head Light.

I recognized Mona as the tearful young woman leaving Auburn's office when I had arrived for my interview. She worshiped Auburn. Lithe and emotional, Mona was unsure of her sexual identity and had sought Auburn's council on the advice of her gynecologist. She threw pots in a stark garret on Exchange Street when she wasn't burning up calories jogging, rowing on Back Cove or churning the waters in the University of Southern Maine pool. My strongest memory of Mona was the asymmetrical smile she'd inappropriately flash when we talked, as if someone were prompting her to hide the sadness written there. As we learned to trust one another, I became Mona's primary confidant and eventually assisted her in severing the umbilical cord that attached her to Auburn.

Doug was fighting throat cancer and, with encouragement from his devoted Greer, seemed to be making progress. He'd had several operations, and spoke through an appliance he held to his throat. His voice was that of a beetle, scratchy and monotonous. Greer clung to Doug's arm, breathing nonstop encouragement into his ear, her long blonde hair billowing over both their shoulders. Auburn had an uphill battle wresting Doug from Greer.

As I listened to their introductions and, later, to their small talk at table, I felt as if we'd all been in the same platoon, fighting an unseen enemy. It was more in their faces than in what they said that tugged at me. I saw the pain in each of their expressions, just as brainwashed prisoners of war show their shame. I looked to Witte for corroboration, but she was busy answering Basil's questions about how we met. At that moment, our history seemed trivial and our future terribly uncertain. I wanted everyone to stop talking and hug each other. We were at war and values had changed.

* * * * * * * *

The picnic went on its superficial way, of course, and I faked my way through the rest of it. Auburn couldn't have called it a success, but she remained magnanimous to the end. I sensed that her disciples were itching to share personal feelings but uncomfortable about doing so in her presence, at least in the group.

Auburn knew her experiment had bombed. Attributing the failure to her breezy picnic format, she remained convinced that a group experience was the right prescription. Desperate to confirm her theory of Universal Love—a concept that, if it had boundaries, might have made sense in our wartime circumstance—she scheduled an all-nighter in an empty storeroom adjacent to her office and inveigled everyone to participate.

Chapter 9

LOCKED UP

By September the Vietnam War was revving up, and I was not surprised to receive a letter from Uncle Sam requesting me to report for my physical. I'd heard that deferments were being given to married fathers and lost no time composing a letter to the draft board. Within a week I received another letter that began: "Dear Proud Father," and went on to list my deferment as 1A. It was signed by Mary Moriarty, Board Clerk. Whooping at the top of our lungs, Witte and I danced around the flat. But my reprieve was short; sides had already been chosen in a private war that would soon consume us.

In a sense, I'd always been at war—with my parents, with myself and, ultimately, with most people I came in contact with. I'd been well trained by Nettie to mistrust everyone. Only innocent animals and engines escaped condemnation, and only engines could be counted on to behave consistently. Raised by a parade of nannies who doubled as Nettie's live-in lovers, in a home saturated with gin and whiskey delivered by the case at the kitchen door, trembling for nineteen years in the shadow of my mother's impending suicide, I sustained life by embracing the cast iron one-cylinder stationary engine while I searched for a woman I could trust. And now, having found her, I didn't trust myself.

Although my sexual orientation was never in question and I considered alcohol poison, I nevertheless had the crawling sensation that I was starting to replicate Nettie by taking terrible risks, making foolish mistakes, and feeling sufficiently worthless about these flaws to contemplate taking my own life. My insecurity had the circular effect of driving me deeper into Auburn's arms, for I was convinced that she alone could cure me.

If Witte had any doubts brewing about my course of salvation, she didn't reveal them; I took that as tacit consent to my continuing therapy. After all, it was Witte who insisted I begin therapy with Dr. Locke in the first place. And so, when Auburn phoned to invite us to a marathon group therapy session on Saturday night, I assumed that Witte would be agreeable, and accepted.

When I hung up, Witte spoke from the couch. Her ragg sweater was hiked to her right shoulder, and Pattin was cradled against her bare midriff, dragging on her nipple and patting the exposed mountain of flesh above it. "What, exactly, did I just agree to, Karcher?" Her tone surprised me.

"That was Dr. Locke calling about a group session."

"So I gathered. What and when? And why wasn't I consulted?"

"Take it easy, Witte. Dr. Locke thinks it would be a good idea to expose me—us—to group therapy. She thinks it will expand our consciousness and help our communication, our relationship."

"Communication? Our relationship? We talk and understand each other. What more could she ask?"

"Why are you so hostile? You're the one who thought I should get help. Remember?"

"Yes, *you* should, and you are. Where do I come into it?"

"You're my wife. Part of my problem is relating to you, in case you hadn't noticed."

"Don't get testy with me, Karcher. Your problems relatin' to others started long before you met me. It's somethin' you've got to work out yourself."

"And I suppose you think you play no part in it?"

"'Course not."

"Wrong. Dr. Locke feels you're too controlling, that I take direction from you as if you were my mother."

"You're problem is not with me, Karcher. It's with your head. You're still takin' orders from Nettie."

The veracity of Witte's accusation cut like a razor. I slumped into a chair and buried my face in my hands. It seemed hopeless. Nothing I said seemed to make any sense. I was inexorably slipping away from her and, so it seemed, from reality. Maybe in a day or two after she cooled off, she'd go along with the group thing. I didn't dare tell her it was to be an all-nighter.

* * * * * * * *

Ida had given us a papoose sling to haul Pattin around in when we went for walks. It could be used across the back or on the chest. Witte, accustomed to a forward moment for so many months, preferred the chest carry. I, on the other hand, slung her over my shoulder. On long walks we took turns. The motion invariably lulled Pattin to sleep within a quarter mile, and we'd be free of her dreadful caterwauling until feeding time.

As the tension mounted between us, our walks became longer. Every nice evening Witte had off we'd set out after supper across the Million Dollar Bridge toward South Portland. Walking seemed to loosen Witte's tongue and ease my pain. We brought wedges of Gruyere, raisins, semi-sweet chocolate bits and grape juice mostly to refuel Witte, who was being drained by Pattin every four hours.

It was during our walk on Friday night that Witte, without prompting, broached the subject. We were on our way home in a dense fog after an especially nostalgic interlude overlooking Casco Bay, listening to the mournful dialog between the Cape Elizabeth diaphone and the Portland Head Light horn. I was still too choked up to talk, remembering my adolescent romp with Bente on the rocks at Two Lights beneath the diaphone's horrendous roar. That was the first time since Nettie weaned me that I'd touched a woman's breasts.

"Karcher, I've been thinking about that group therapy session tomorrow. I'll go along to support you, if that's what you want. But that's all."

"Sorry, my mind was wandering. What did you say?"

"I said, I'll go with you tomorrow, if you need me."

"I'd really appreciate it. I'm sure the group could benefit from the clarity of your thinking."

"Thinking is a silent process, Karcher."

"Okay, okay, you don't have to say a thing. I'd just feel better if you were there."

"Don't suppose they'll appreciate Pattin's presence."

"They'll love her. Besides, she'll be asleep most of the time."

"I'll sit near the door in case she cries."

"Good idea."

The dueling fog signals faded to bovine moans as we approached the bridge. Ahead, the waterfront lights began to pop like flash bulbs from the haze. As we paced in silence I watched Witte from the corner of my eye. Unburdened by Pattin, who was fast asleep on my back, she strode erect, leading with her chin. Her elastic waist had nearly shrunk to its former girth, and the roll and sway had returned to her gait, urging her unbridled hair to sweep and undulate. While she still moved with a sensual self-assurance that made my groin ache, her stride had lost some of its snap.

Witte was no longer a girl; she bore the burdens of womanhood. But there was more than mature solemnity in her expression that night. I saw under the diffused saffron glow of Portland's street lamps Ida's tragic mask: long and conflicted but facing life squarely. Like her mother, Witte would endure any pain so long as it was legitimate, but that left few horizontal lines in her face.

* * * * * * * *

We were the first to arrive at Auburn's den at ten of eight on Saturday evening. The session was due to begin at eight sharp. When Witte wasn't looking, I'd tucked a few extra diapers into our baby pack along with a supply of snacks, so we three could last the night. The girls had just emerged from the tub, dusted with scented talc and smelling delicious. Auburn gave us both a warm hug, cooed politely over Pattin and directed us to a bare room at the end of the hall. She stayed behind to greet the others.

Witte stopped at the storeroom door to scan the circle of nine pillows centered on its barren, heart-pine floor, the wrought iron grill over its only window, the naked light bulb dangling from its cord and the heavy latch striker on the door jamb beside her.

The room was perhaps twenty feet square with a twelve foot embossed tin ceiling painted battleship gray. Uninviting as it appeared, the aroma of machine oil and cast iron put my mind at ease.

"This place looks like a prison, Karcher. I don't like it."

"Must have been a machine shop or a tool crib. Reminds me of your dad's power house."

"Yes, but there's nothin' in it." Witte shuddered and refused to follow me inside.

"There's pillows," I said, flopping down on one.

"Where's the bathroom?"

"Just down the hall on your right. It's non-denominational, but it's clean."

Witte edged into the room with Pattin hiccuping on her shoulder and stood near the door with her back to the wall. "I'll be here if you need me, dear."

"You're not going to stand there all night, are you?" I immediately regretted my revealing question, but before Witte could answer, in walked Harry and Porcher.

"God, will you get a load of this," Harry opened, arms spread, gesturing to the empty walls. "Looks like a detox cell. Hey, looky here. Yours, Karcher?" Pattin gurgled and blew a bubble of saliva as she reached for Harry's glasses. Witte stood her ground in proud silence.

"Yup. I just hope she doesn't fuss."

Porcher was examining Pattin from several angles as if she were judging a show dog. "Cute little thing. What formula do you use?"

"Pattin's a joint venture, and she feeds right here." She cupped her free breast for emphasis.

"Well, good for you," Porcher encouraged. "She'll be the healthier for it. Would you like me to hold her while you find a seat?"

Witte let Porcher take Pattin from her, then addressed me. "Karcher, throw me that pillow. Yuh, that big blue one." I took from the circle the cushion she indicated and placed it below where she was standing. She settled demurely on it and reached up to relieve Porcher of our little doll, whose lower lip had begun to quiver.

Auburn returned with the others in tow and directed us to fill in the circle. Her husband, Basil, was conspicuously absent. When she closed the heavy oak door behind us, it latched with the final authority of a bank vault.

Fred did not sit, but paced the perimeter of the room, looking very uncomfortable. When he came to Witte, he gave her a wide berth and diverted his eyes. The rest of us took our places. I sat on a cushion at one end of the break in the circle with my back to Witte and facing Auburn.

"Fred, come sit over here by me." Auburn patted the pillow on her right. "Aren't you going to join us, Witte?"

"Figured I'd stay close to the door, 'case she starts to holler."

Remembering how Nettie always insisted that I sit in a circle on the floor, Indian-style, equidistant from her and Bente during her frequent "councils of war," I edged my cushion to close the gap and shut Witte out. Fred finally took his designated seat, folding his legs awkwardly in front of him, and Auburn began.

"Karcher, that was a significant move you just made. Can you tell us your motive?"

All eyes in the circle were suddenly upon me. "I...I just figured you wanted us to sit in a circle, judging from the way the cushions were laid out. And since I'd broken the circle by moving a cushion for Witte, I thought I'd better fix it."

"Why did you wait until Witte declined to join us, then?"

I could feel my ears getting red. Why was Auburn attacking me, and in front of all these people? "I dunno; maybe I'm kinda pissed she won't be a part of the group."

"Good, Karcher. Harry, you look confused. How does all this strike you?"

"I want to know the structure of this meeting. Seems to me we've gotten off to a bad start. Aren't you going to give us an agenda?"

"There isn't any structure, Harry. What goes on in this session is up to you all. I'm just here as your guide and referee. Now, can you tell us how you feel about Karcher's closing Witte out of the circle?"

"Seems she closed herself out. It's not Karcher's fault. I think it's kinda shitty that you're picking on him."

"Do you agree with that, Mona?"

Mona was sitting diagonally across from me, looking at the floor directly in front of her. She drew little hearts in the dust with the tip of her finger while she answered without looking up. "I don't like this; it's hostile as hell. You want me to choose sides."

Porcher couldn't keep still any longer. "Let's cut the crap. This is going nowhere. Witte has a baby to care for, for Chris-sake."

Fred started to get up but Auburn stayed his arm. On my right, Greer was comforting an obviously distressed Doug. Auburn was smiling and nodding approval; she began again.

"Okay. I think it's time we mixed things up. Karcher, I'd like you to swap places with Mona and sit here, next to me. Fred, you stay put. You, too, Harry. Doug, please move left one cushion and take Greer's place. Greer can sit next to Fred, displacing Porcher, who will fill Doug's vacant cushion. There."

As I settled next to her, Auburn winked and squeezed my hand while the others were in transit. My thrill was canceled by a bolt of terror when I realized that Witte could have been watching, but a furtive glance put my mind at ease; she was playing with Pattin, who had a fist grip on her pinky. When everyone had found their new places, Auburn justified the move.

"My purpose in moving you around is to equalize the energy and foster independent thinking. With old alliances broken, new ones can form that may be helpful."

Abrasive as Brillo and with hair to match, Porcher butted in: "When are you going to start the music, Auburn?"

Greer, behaving like a nurse unfairly separated from her primary patient, spoke up for the first time. "When I took the oath, 'in sickness or in health, till death do us part,' I considered it a bond for life, not something to be taken lightly."

"Jeezus, Greer!" Harry exploded, "You're only six feet from him; it's just a temporary separation." Harry looked at Auburn and received a nod of approval.

All I could feel was the heat from Auburn's body. She was so close, I could smell the smoke adsorbed by her blouse. If I leaned right, her gravity would drop me square in her lap and I'd be engulfed in her flames. I wanted to fall. Oh, how I wanted to burn. I swayed left and right to confirm that I wasn't really heavier on her side. Auburn must have sensed my ardor, for she placed her hand on my thigh and held it there a moment in confirmation before addressing the group.

"Now, I'd like you to close your eyes and breathe slowly. Become aware of the person on either side of you. Feel their presence. Send them a telepathic message if you wish. Be receptive to incoming communications."

Auburn drew an enormous breath, closed her eyes and exhaled forever through her nose. I watched her chest slowly fall until she slumped forward, limp and still. Then I followed suit.

At first all I could get was an image of Auburn purring in my arms. I felt dizzy and feared I might execute the right fall in full view of Witte, who I was sure was scrutinizing me. But my torso was stiffened by a chill in my left shoulder. The odor of damp dog and sweat that followed, forced my eyes open.

Porcher, wearing rank denim hog washers and work boots, was glaring up at me. Her square face, set with small, bark-brown eyes, was so repulsive, I snapped my eyes shut and tried tuning in on the others. Nothing came but footage of Porcher attacking me with a studded choke collar that she whirled overhead as she advanced. Thankfully, Auburn called off the trance before Porcher's chain hit its mark.

"Okay, when you're ready, open your eyes and remember your thoughts."

I neither wanted to open my eyes nor remember my thoughts, and held on for another minute while the others came to. When the scuffling and sighing reached all points of the circle I knew I had to join them and opened my eyes. Auburn had been watching me for her cue to resume.

"Anyone care to tell us about their experience?"

Without thinking, I blurted: "Yeah. It's weird. With my eyes closed I became acutely aware of the women on either side of me but of no one else. Auburn, on my right, warm and nurturing; Porcher, on my left, cold and accusing. I felt drawn to the one and repulsed by the other." I didn't admit to opening my eyes mid-seance.

"Can you ascribe any meaning to the experience, Karcher?" Auburn was coaching with obvious delight. I heard Porcher expel a hiss of contempt, but she didn't interrupt. The others looked on with rapt attention.

"I'm not sure, but I think it's got something to do with my relationship with my mother. She's gone, of course, but I'm still trying to deal with her duality."

"You mean, her acting like both a man and a woman?"

"Yes. I wanted her to act more like Auburn, here, not like Porcher."

Harry took my cue and entered the fray. "I can relate to that."

"That's enough out of you." Porcher's face was crimson, and her mouth resembled that of a fish between breaths. "You're not around enough to know who I am."

Fred again started to get up. This time it was Greer, on his right, who coaxed him down, whispering loud enough for everyone to hear. "It's okay, Fred. They're only sparring in jest."

"Think I'm kidding?" Porcher continued. "This turkey plays in shit all day and most of the night and then has the gall to call me a dyke."

Harry looked desperately at Auburn for assistance, but Auburn was paying attention to Fred, who was frozen white and shaking. I took advantage of the change in focus to check on Witte. She had given over her cushion to Pattin and was sitting on the bare floor, back against the wall, hugging her knees, taking in the whole scene with her huge gray eyes. Her mouth was an almost invisible dash beneath her long nose. I sent assurance with my eyes, but she didn't move a muscle. Pattin slept soundly within radiant reach of her warmth.

I knew the group experience wasn't setting well with Witte, but I felt I should ride it out and take her gaff later. Little did I know then, less than an hour into the session, how close to boiling over she was.

By now, Fred was crying and being simultaneously comforted first by Auburn and Greer, then by Mona and Doug. Harry and Porcher remained in place, glaring at each other across the circle. I moved to assist the others with Fred and heard for the first time his pathetic, barely audible sobs for help.

"I...I can't take it anymore. There's nothing but h..hate following me. Nobody c...cares about anyone else. I j...just wanna die." He paused and looked up with the eyes of a bloodhound, focused far beyond us. "See, sh...she's gonna leave me, j...just like Becky. They don't care about me, j...just themselves."

"That's not true, and you know it, honey," soothed Auburn in her best imitation of Mae West. "We're all here with you because we care about you, Fred. We love you, very much." We all murmured in agreement and took turns hugging him as best we could. Although I hardly knew Fred, I found myself moved to tears at his plight. He was a goner, beyond recall, but I didn't want to let him go, for fear that his defeat might be mine.

We were thus engaged in trying to heal Fred, a tearful people pile, writhing with his pain, when my arm was forcefully arrested. Startled, I looked up to see Witte standing over me, blazing with rage.

"This has gone far enough." Almost single-handedly she lifted me from my kneeling position and addressed Auburn.

"You may be helpin' Karcher individually, but you're certainly not doing him any good here. We're goin' home."

Auburn mustered her best control. "I'm sorry you feel threatened by Karcher's progress, Witte. I know it must make you uncomfortable to watch group therapy from a distance. It takes participation to understand the process. Perhaps you'll choose to join us next time." She forced a saccharine smile. "You see, when one person in a relationship grows and the other is left behind, it becomes uncomfortable for the static one."

"There isn't going to *be* a next time. You're manipulatin' these people — and *my* husband — to discard the boundaries that protect them from each other. That's dangerous. Look at the mess you've made. I hope you're competent enough to put everyone back together." She marched over to Pattin and shouldered her in one scoop. "You comin', Karcher?"

I was too shocked to protest and more than a little afraid of Witte's anger, which had never surfaced to this extent before. Steeped as I was in Auburn's quagmire of Universal Love, I had forgotten that I lived with Loring's daughter, a woman with cast iron integrity that tolerated no deception. Dodging Auburn's smooth entreaties, I hastily excused myself and followed Witte out the door.

Chapter 10

SNOWBALL

The memory of Auburn's all-nighter still burned white hot in December as if it had just occurred. It was fueled by the dreadful silence that followed us home and dwelled for weeks at 157b Pine Street, the sight of Witte's facial muscles locked in bitter conflict, the incessant groaning of the Cape Elizabeth diaphone during our invariably fog-shrouded walks, and Pattin's pitiful cries of insecurity between feedings. My guilt peaked a week later and continued to torment me long after Witte and I reestablished communication in early October. Ironically, it was Auburn who moved us off bottom dead center.

My weekly sessions with Auburn were allowed to continue unchallenged for the duration of the fall, but I knew it wasn't tacit approval on Witte's part; it was grim tolerance. Witte stuck to a decision until her evidence no longer supported it. In this case she felt she had insufficient evidence against Auburn for a conviction. But I sensed that her docket was getting full. I knew my days with Auburn were numbered.

For most of our meetings following the marathon, Auburn and I dissected the group experience and tried to plumb its effect both on our relationship as well as on my marriage. It was clear from the start that changes had to be made for my survival; the silent conflict at home was destroying me. I was in no mood for cuddling, let alone petting, and Auburn did not push her advantage. By maintaining clinical distance between us I was able to make good use of her perceptive observations. Under Witte's fire, Auburn became an insightful therapist.

"Karcher," she said to me the week before Thanksgiving, "I've noticed you mist up whenever we discuss your mother. I think you love her very much in spite of the way she behaved. You never had a mother-child relationship with her, and I think you have really been in mourning for that."

"So you think I see you as a mother figure and love you as I wanted to love Nettie?"

"That's part of it."

"Then what about Witte? Who does she represent?"

"All that you missed in Nettie."

"Then she's just like you, a surrogate mother."

"No. Witte—I hate to admit it—is a sexual stimulus for you; something that no mother, especially one of Nettie's orientation, could provide."

"But I feel attracted to you, now."

"Not in the same sense, perhaps. I think you *want* to offer me sexual favors, but something blocks you from acting. What is it that prevents you from letting go?"

"Guilt, I suppose. Loyalty to Witte." (I didn't dare admit, even to myself, that I found Auburn too plump.) "Maybe if I stopped trying so hard."

"Lovemaking should never be forced, Karcher." She paused and frowned. "But it's your relationship with Witte that we need to concentrate on; ours can simmer on the back burner for awhile. I'll always be here for you."

I didn't have to make a choice after all, or so it seemed under Auburn's gracious guidance. I could love them both, each in a different and very special way. Auburn's doctrine of Universal Love eased my guilt, allowing me to consider Witte my seductress instead of my conscience.

Filled with hope, I returned home that night determined to derail the deadlock between us. There was a birch fire crackling in the fireplace, and Witte was prone on the couch with her rosebud flannel nightshirt hiked so that it barely covered her rump. Her toes were hooked over one armrest and her hair was draped over the other. She was reading Nettie's tattered edition of *A Hat-Tub Tale*, which she had borrowed from Friends and Relations on our honeymoon. When she saw me, she flipped to a seated position, drew her legs under her and squealed with excitement.

"I can't wait till Pattin's old enough, so I can read this to her, dear. It's about this adorable, selfless bear, Tuck, who has a spoon paw and a fork paw for making salads, and the irascible rat, Nip, she rescues from the Bay of Fundy, who has a fish hook at the end of his tail. They..."

"I know it well," I interrupted. "Nettie read it to me often. How do you think she got the names for the privies on the island: Nip for the boys and Tuck for the girls?"

As I spoke of the book, a wave of bittersweet nostalgia swept over me. "Hey, I've got it. Let's spend this weekend at Loonwater. We haven't been to the island since our honeymoon. There should be plenty of wood left if the hunters didn't take it."

Not surprisingly, my first attempt at a reconciliation met stony resistance. Witte's face fell to a scowl, and she shook her head vigorously, which sent her unbridled hair roiling like a thunderhead. When her seething cloud of diesel-brown silk settled, she swept it out of her face before answering through clenched teeth.

"What honeymoon?"

"You really know how to hurt a guy."

"Karcher, it's November and twenty degrees out."

"I can move the stove in Pooh's and stuff the pipe up the fireplace chimney. We'll have plenty of heat. It'll be real cozy."

"It's too soon to go back there. You'll go to pieces and I'll have two dependents. Besides, the lake is skimmin' over."

"I have a safety net now. Remember?"

"Don't push it, Karcher. You've enough to deal with here."

"Look, I know you don't think much of Dr. Locke, but she's really wonderful in private, one-on-one therapy. I've learned a lot about myself in our individual sessions."

"And a lot about her, I'll warrant."

"Just what in hell do you mean by that?"

"I mean, Karcher, that I don't trust the woman. She's a manipulator."

"What is it you want, Witte? For me to get well, or for me to leave you? It's been like a loony bin here for months, ever since the group: you brooding in silence; Pattin screaming for attention; and me skulking about in terror, waiting for you to blow. I've had it. It's time we hashed this out, once and for all."

"You're in love with her."

"You mean, I'm experiencing transference. Sure, it's a part of the process."

"No, you're in love with her."

"That's ridiculous, Witte. I love Auburn as I love a savior; I'm deeply grateful to her. She's like the mother I wish I'd had."

"Applesauce! The symptoms of being in love and lovin' someone are different. You don't go around with a glazed look, barking and rocking the shopping cart for your mother. I want you to stop seein' her."

"And what would that accomplish?"

"For one, we'd be on equal ground. With you off cloud nine, we might have a chance to fix this before it's broke for good."

"Witte, I'm in love with *you*, not Auburn." I moved to sit beside her, but she jumped up and strode into the kitchen, indignant and intent on retaining her space.

I followed her as far as the breakfast table and tried again. "She's just a figurehead in my life at present, setting my course straight in the storm."

"From what I've seen of her navigatin', she'll run you on the rocks."

"It's not the way it looks, Witte. If I quit now, I'll be throwing away over a year of therapy and hundreds of dollars. Is that what you really want?"

"If you don't quit, you'll soon be alone. I know her kind of woman; they milk you dry then give you the boot. And when it's over, you won't have me to come home to."

"Witte, this is preposterous. You're working yourself into a lather for nothing. I want you to make an appointment with her. Ask her about what's going on, express all your fears, and if you still feel my therapy is destructive, I'll find someone else—a man, if you like—to take over."

"Maybe." Witte's mouth became a dot. The subject was closed. I'd squeaked through this time. Small miracle.

* * * * * * * *

Determined to convince her of my devotion and with the challenge of our aborted honeymoon refreshed, I prevailed upon Witte to break for Loonwater on Saturday. She agreed to one overnight. I wanted two, but she won out. WGAN was forecasting unsettled weather for Saturday night and early Sunday; so, we piled the Ford's back seat to the roof with wool sweaters, parkas, boots, buntings, diapers, water jugs and food for a week.

Witte believed in being prepared for the worst. "We might get snowed in, Karcher," she announced grimly, "and if the lake skims hard, we may have to bridge the gut and walk out. You have enough lumber over there to deck a catwalk?"

"We'll use the Grumman canoe; it can chop through anything."

With thirty weight oil still in the Ford, the starter spun lazily in the grip of a Portland November morning, but the engine caught, as always, on the second churn and shook off the chill by the time we reached the Forest Avenue intersection on Congress Street. Pattin was wedged upright between us and, to my amazement, was gurgling contentedly despite having been mummified rigid by all the wraps Witte insisted on placing around her. Navigation was tricky with the back light and rear quarter windows blacked out with our gear, but Witte kept watch on the right, and I did my best to decipher the trembling images flashing across the outside mirror. Together we managed to avoid scraping anything. We had a ten minute wait at the farm for Dan's cows to finish crossing the gravel fire lane; one, who mistook the deep ruts for a grating and repeatedly refused to cross, absorbed most of the time and Dan's attention, much to Witte's amusement.

"That poor dear's so scared she won't give Dan a drop come sundown."

Witte laughed until the tears ran down her cheeks. So infectious was her mirth that I, too, began laughing. Poor Pattin didn't know what to make of us and began to howl, which made us laugh all the harder. Animals, I've found, are consummate stress relievers, and we were both prime candidates for cow therapy.

"You know," she said, picking up Pattin, "we ought to have a puppy—a comical breed, like a Saint Bernard." (She pronounced it Ber'-nerd.)

"In the city?"

"No, silly. When we move out here." She gestured to the boathouse, now dead ahead, whose weathered upright cedar logs drew our attention to the towering pines and the lake beyond. "Wouldn't be hard to fix it up; we could do it mostly ourselves."

The thought of making a nest in the boathouse ignited simultaneous joy and terror, for while there was nothing I wanted more than to move back to the lake, a large dark part of my heart shuddered at the thought of being trapped there with all the memories, to say nothing of what Nettie would think of our renovating one of her buildings. I pulled the Model A to a stop and sat speechless behind the wheel, staring at the scene before me, noting the roof thickly thatched with pine spills that should have been swept off, the blackened and rotting feet of the logs where the snow had been left to pile up, the crumbling screens, the sagging doors, the broken latch. I could never keep it up like Nettie. No one could.

My anxiety was exacerbated by Auburn's distance from the lake. If I lived in the boathouse, would she be able to reach me in time should I start to spiral? Although Witte had demonstrated competence at putting me back together on our honeymoon, she wasn't a doctor and couldn't prescribe tranquilizers. And more and more, it was Auburn and not Witte I envisioned living with.

Witte pushed in the ignition plunger and the engine rolled slowly to a stop. "Come on, Karcher. I need some exercise to chase this chill." She opened the door and started to get out.

It was getting to be a habit with her, to kill the engine when I was at the wheel and she wanted my attention. Just then I needed to hear the secure putter of the Ford's four cylinders idling and resented her censoring it. "I wish you'd keep your hands off the key when I'm driving, Witte."

"You're not drivin' and I'm cold."

"I'll decide when to shut down the engine, damn it."

Witte re-closed the door and looked at me in disbelief. "What now, Karcher? One minute you're laughing and the next you're snapping. I thought you wanted to do this."

"I do. I just don't like you cuing my every move. If you're in such a hurry to work up a sweat, lug some of this stuff you insisted on bringing down to the shore. I'll watch Pattin and collect my thoughts a moment."

"Suit yourself."

Witte thrust open the door and hiked herself out in one flounce to illustrate her indignation. Without bothering to close her door, she flung open the back door on her side, grabbed an armload of clothing and marched for the lake, puffing frosty clouds ahead of her, as proud and determined a figurehead as any man could carve.

I reached over my sleeping daughter and pulled the door closed. How could I explain the turmoil in my heart to Witte? Life for her ran with the predictable direction of a locomotive; it took a significant obstacle to derail it. Mine, by contrast, fluttered with the constancy of a mayfly, blown between gloom and ecstasy, unable to land.

After Witte's third round trip, I felt foolish and lugged the water jugs and boxes of food to the beach. The lake was still and silver gray. I poked at its surface to check for ice; the ripples from my hand ran out unchecked. I strained to detect the whisper of slush in the north cove, but all that reached my ears were two desolate croaks from a raven winging west and the sound of Witte's trudging.

A moment later Witte pulled up alongside with the last of our duffel. "Sky looks angry, Karcher. Awful still. Better get across before the lake kicks up."

Nettie's eighteen-foot Grumman canoe looked like it had seen service on Midway Island. Peppered with patch-welded bullet holes received the winter she'd left it on the main cabin porch when the hunters used it for target practice, the bluff but capacious tin can tracked well enough when loaded but left an embarrassing wake, especially under the urge of two paddlers trying to keep warm. Pattin, in her little life jacket, nestled between the soft luggage, batted at the hollow center thwart above her and took obvious pleasure at the gonging she created.

"Shush, Pattin. You'll scare the fish, dear," Witte mocked from the bow between sinuous sweeps of her paddle. Her pull was so strong and her timing so steady that I seldom had to correct our course. If only Nettie could have seen her at work like this.

"Bow engine, neutral," I called as we neared the landing. Witte pulled her paddle, spun it dry across her knees and stowed it ahead of her as we glided noiselessly toward shore. Then the hiss of sand under the bow, and we were aground. I braced the canoe with my paddle while Witte jumped ashore and pulled us higher on the beach. Pattin and I went ahead to open Pooh's. Inside, I propped her in the snowshoe rocker and ran a line around her so she wouldn't fall if she squirmed.

The Brown log stove was an easy shove into place before the hearth. Fortunately, this time there was plenty of dry wood left on the porch, and within minutes a satisfying crackle of white pine twigs and birch bark emanated from within its cast iron box. Pattin appeared mesmerized by the orange flicker at the draft window and quickly fell asleep, her tiny head slumped forward over the rope that bound her to the chair, her mittened miniature hands slowly opening and closing as she dreamed.

When Witte arrived with the first load, the cabin was already beginning to feel the stove's warmth. The thump of the log door closing awakened Pattin, and she started caterwauling. Witte took one look at her and turned to scold me through her smile.

"You trying to strangle our daughter?"

Ignoring the icicle poking at my heart, I helped Witte untie Pattin and suggested she sit by the stove while I finished hauling the gear. She settled into the snowshoe rocker, stripped some of Pattin's garb and prepared to feed her. The peaceful expression I saw on both their faces as I left clashed hideously with my torment.

Auburn would understand these feelings. She'd be at my side now, taking my emotional temperature, soothing, coaxing with just the right words to set my mind at ease, instead of sitting like a bump on a log by the fire, oblivious of my needs and responding only to our daughter's cry.

Even the sky seemed to be more attuned to my state than Witte. I watched from the landing the disgruntled gray clouds punching at the faster moving white ones that came within reach. And still there wasn't a breath of air. The battle was a way off yet, raging far above us, but I knew it was only a matter of time before the arena moved to ground zero at Loonwater.

It took me four round trips to lug the remaining stuff to Pooh's. Not wanting to chill the cabin, I stacked everything on the porch before entering. Witte was just putting Pattin down on the cot.

"I need her change bag, dear. And some water, so I can warm her bath. She's messed her pants. Yes, you, you little stinker."

I dragged the two chamber pots from under the bed and headed once more for the lake. At the head of the path a red squirrel taunted cheekily and scampered under the porch. Nettie would have gone for her gun to save the bedding. I looked back at the roof with its fresh layer of pine spills awaiting ignition from the sparks leaving the chimney, and felt ashamed. I'd failed again to make camp this year.

When I returned, Witte held open the screen door for me to pass, then let it slam. She shut the log door firmly and set its wooden latch. The double impact was sufficient to dislodge the padlock from the precarious perch I'd given it on the lintel. It fell to the floor—"thock"—and that started the tape loop going inside my head.

"Did you forget something, Witte?"

Witte was moving to retrieve the lock when my question arrested her. "No, dear. What?" She stooped to pick it up.

"Is that the way you were taught to close a door?"

Witte straightened with the padlock in her hand. Her forehead furrowed as her eyes searched mine. For a moment I thought she was going to cry, as if she was nine years old, responding to a reprimand from her father. The corners of her mouth sagged and her lips began to tremble, but she composed herself with indignation.

"Save your Nettie reincarnations for Dr. Locke, Karcher." Without diverting her glare she placed the padlock on the window sill adjacent to the door.

"It belongs above the door, Witte."

"Outside, Mister!"

Witte reopened the door and again held the screen open. When I hesitated, my grim gatekeeper pointed and widened the aperture of her stormy eyes. The thrust of her chest as she stood at attention, which would in peacetime have triggered a tremor in my groin, intimidated me so that I obediently pulled on my coat and slid past her. She followed me onto the porch, pulled the door closed behind her and defiantly slammed the screen. This time there was no echo; the padlock stayed put.

"You want my reaction?"

Witte was shaking with rage. Without waiting for my answer, she advanced, hauled off and dealt me a stinging blow on the cheek, stepped back and read me my rights.

"Now, either you act civil or we girls go. I'm not on trial here. Get ahold of yourself."

I was as astonished by her summation as I was by her attack, and stood, stunned, with my hand to my cheek. She searched my face for a moment, breathing loudly through her nose, then snapped an about face and returned to the warmth of the cabin.

Nettie would have handled the situation differently, but no one could have made more sense with so few words. Witte had me dead in her sights. The war was on and we hadn't even had lunch.

* * * * * * * *

It was beginning to look like we were in for a substantial storm. The sky had turned a uniform slate color, and a breeze had come up from the northeast, but I couldn't go back inside, not right away. To kill time and assuage my guilt I dragged the ladder from under the porch, propped it against the eave, grabbed the broom by the door and ascended to sweep the roof. By the time I'd finished clearing the pine spills from the north slope, the first fine flakes of snow began to tickle my nose. I bent to the broom in earnest and had the other side clear before the snow started to stick. Before descending to face Witte, I heaved several deep breaths.

"We're going to get it," I observed, shaking the snow from my parka at the door. "The gulls on the breakwater are silent, scrunched down and all pointing northeast."

Witte had her back to me and was turning out a can of lentil soup into one of the battered pots we'd brought. The wash water was already simmering. She spoke to the hearth.

"You hungry?"

"Sure am," I said, trying to sound cheerful.

"Bread's in that carton; ham and cheese in the cooler. Make mine with two slices of cheese and lots of mayonnaise."

"You never eat cheese, Witte." I began rummaging for the sandwich ingredients.

Without looking up, she snapped, "Do, here."

I decided against asking whether she wanted lettuce and made hers without, poured us both a glass of milk, took a seat at the table under the porch windows and began munching, hoping that I'd guessed wrong. I wanted to hurt her for being the one in my cabin instead of Auburn.

Witte poured the soup, slid a bowl in front of me and sat at the opposite end of the table. She eyeballed me quickly then looked down at her sandwich. I waited for the complaint, but she ate in silence, her steel gray eyes focused on the building storm.

"Didn't know whether you liked lettuce or not."

She waited to answer until the sandwich was consumed and her mouth was completely empty.

"Lot you don't know about me, Karcher."

Witte delivered her line leaning forward as far as her chest and the table would allow, aiming her scowl directly at me like a great horned owl hooting at its mate.

Anxious as I was to trip her up, I was at a complete loss to answer such a profound charge, let alone counter with heavier artillery. Better to say nothing than exacerbate the situation. But it made me boil to let her win so easily.

I sat back in my chair as if the impact of her round had knocked me there. My mind's gears whirred impotently, trying to mine a retort that would put her down, but all I could think of was how much I wanted to punch her in the nose. How dare she sass me here, at Loonwater. Nettie would never have put up with it. She'd have had an atomic answer for Witte that would end the war in one blast. Why couldn't I do that?

The problem with Witte was that she had a perfect sense of priority. There was no rational defense against her logic. So I had to be irrational.

Of course. Remembering how upset she had become when Bente propositioned her on Christmas eve, the plan became obvious. Act crazy enough and she'll fall apart and I'll win. That shouldn't be hard; I'd been tutored at home by the best. If I played it right, I could drive her crazy without driving her away. I wanted to destroy her, not lose her. I shuddered at my sinister plot and hoped that Witte couldn't see the devilish glint in my eye.

"When will you start believing that she's gone, Karcher?" Witte sighed and rose to clear the dishes.

"Gone? No way. Nettie's right here in this room."

"That's enough!" The dishes clattered into the wash pot, but Witte's remark that followed had a fainter ring. "No one with a midge of sense believes in ghosts."

I could tell by the flattening of her inflection that she was struggling. It reminded me of her reaction in the kitchen of Friends and Relations on our honeymoon night. Not that she was superstitious, any more than I; it was more discomposure than fear, but I could use it to my advantage.

"It's like I'm hearing her voice when you speak. When we were last here, I kept seeing her in your place. This time it's just her voice."

"Good. Then she's on her way out of our lives."

She said 'our lives.' I still had a lever. "Ever since we got here," I lied, "your speech pattern has been identical to hers, your brusque manner the same. It's more than coincidence."

Witte swallowed hard and moved to sit on the bed. Her color had faded, but she kept up a good front. "If you're tryin' to scare me, forget it."

"The woman I married had compassion, but she disappeared and was replaced by a clone of my mother. Am I cursed to live forever by Nettie's rules?"

"You baby bastard!" Witte was on her feet again and coming for me, swinging. I rose and grabbed her wrists in time, but I hadn't anticipated the anger in her legs. Her right heel came down hard on my left instep, then her left knee found my groin. I sank to the floor and folded up in agony. The pain was so excruciating that I blacked out for a few seconds. When I came to, the purlins and pine knots were swirling above me, Witte's face was a blur and Pattin was howling. I nearly lost my lunch before the cabin came to rest and my eyes were again able to focus. Witte was kneeling over me and quaking like an aspen leaf. I hoped it was out of remorse.

"*Now* you deserve compassion." Her voice quavered with rage. "But not from me."

Unable to move, I watched her leave my side and lift Pattin into her arms. As I lay there reflecting on what had happened, I came to the inescapable conclusion that Nettie, tough as she was, couldn't hold a candle to Witte when it came to discipline.

As soon as her temper had cooled, Witte began glancing anxiously in my direction as she bathed Pattin. Her brow was knitted and her eyes bespoke a torment deeper even than her mother's. I wanted to comfort her, tell her I was okay, that I deserved her wrath and admired her guts, but each time I tried to move, someone stuck a knife in my testes.

When Pattin was clean and contentedly patting the ovoid bed-warming stones on the hearth, Witte returned to my side, lay on the floor and pressed herself against my back. I could feel her body convulse as she held me and sobbed into my nape. She said nothing, and neither did I.

Pattin soon found us and took great glee in pulling our noses, first mine then Witte's, until we were lifted from our chasm by her infectious mirth. Small children have restorative powers second only to animals.

When I could crawl without screaming, the three of us took up residence on the bed and cuddled away the remainder of the afternoon and evening while the snow wrapped Pooh's in a blanket of eider down.

Witte kept the fire going overnight and let me sleep. By morning my convalescence had progressed to the point where I could walk, but shoveling snow was out of the question. Sensing my delicate condition, Witte didn't press me for help. Pattin was placed in my arms while she shuffled about, quilt wrapped, fixing us oatmeal and eggs. When breakfast was over, she bade me rest awhile longer. Although I could see that she had had little sleep, I didn't argue.

"Can you watch her while I clear a path, dear?"

"Sure.

"Unless she kicks me," I added, trying not to laugh.

Chapter 11

KARCHER'S MOON

The winter of our discontent was relentless. Ever since Witte dug us out of Pooh's and freed the Ford so we could slither back along Dan's fire road, the snow had hardly let up. Confinement led to confrontation, and our rift grew ever wider. Not that there weren't compensating moments.

One was on a Sunday morning in February, 1962. After a rare night of passion, Witte emerged from the bathroom and announced, "Nature's perverse. I gag on my goddamn toothbrush but not on you."

"Try brushing your tongue before bed instead of after breakfast," I suggested. We both laughed, easing our stress sufficiently to tear some more at the net that entangled us.

"Did you make an appointment with Dr. Locke yet, Witte?" I knew she hadn't.

"'Course not."

"Then you're satisfied with the way my therapy is going?"

"Don't put words in my mouth, Karcher. You know darn well how I feel about that woman."

"Okay, but you've got to admit that she's been able to help me."

"Help what? Your attraction to heavy women?"

"You're a real crusher."

"What did you call me? Crusher?"

"Yes, as in stone."

"Very funny, Karcher. Look, we're losin' ground with this lady friend of yours. We need a marriage counselor, not a hippotherapist."

"Do you know what you just called her?"

"Yuh. She has an eatin' disorder, Karcher. That's enough to disqualify her from tryin' to cure others, right there."

"She's not fat, Witte, just pleasingly plump. Substantial."

"She's a sow, but you can't see that because you're infatuated. It's disgustin'. Both of you. Makes me sick."

Witte pondered a moment then resumed in a near monotone. "I've had it, Karcher. Competition's too strong. I could handle one woman, maybe, but not two. Nettie's bad enough; every man loves his mother. But this blimp."

"You've got me all wrong. I don't *love* my mother. I *hate* her. That's the problem."

"You don't even know what love is."

* * * * * * * *

That's the way it went on Sunday while the snow piled ever higher outside our basement window. By Monday morning we could hardly see out. Most of Portland was shut down, including my plant. Auburn called at noon to cancel our Wednesday appointment as she had contracted the flu. That left Witte and me trapped together underground before a blazing birch fire, glaring at one another from opposite ends of the couch. It was to be a fight to the finish.

By two, exhaustion had so exaggerated our differences and clouded our ability to reason that, at one point, I suggested we call in Loring and Ida as arbiters.

"You crazy? Daddy and Mumma don't understand infidelity. It'd be like tellin' them you had cancer. They'd freak out."

"I've not been unfaithful, Witte. Nothing has happened. How many times have I to tell you? We didn't do it."

"But you tried. That's enough."

"No, *she* tried. I couldn't get it up."

"But you wanted to. Admit it."

"Yes. Okay. I wanted to. Satisfied?"

"No."

Witte bit her lower lip and shut her eyes tight to block the tears, but they trickled out the corners and began running down her cheeks. She smeared them with the back of her hand, sniffed hard and turned away to watch the fire while she pondered her next move. When she had collected her thoughts, she sat up, blew her nose and faced me. Her jaw muscles rippled as she spoke.

"So, it's okay for you to bang out, but I gotta stay by the hearth. That it?"

"It's not like that, Witte. I'm not one of those guys who goes whoring around. This is a very peculiar relationship."

"I'll say."

Witte was starting to turn crimson, and I was afraid of another onslaught. I had to calm her quickly.

"What I mean is, Dr. Locke and I share things that only develop as the result of a doctor/patient relationship, and that sharing brings us emotionally close to one another."

"That's malpractice, Karcher. The doctor's supposed to remain uninvolved."

"True, ordinarily. But Dr. Locke is an unorthodox psychiatrist who isn't bound by rigid convention. She uses creative techniques tailored to each individual's needs. This is one that she's found helpful in cases such as mine."

"Yes, techniques designed to ensure that her patients become totally dependent on her. You're brainwashed, Karcher, and can't see what she's done to you."

Witte threw her head back and groaned. Her eyes began searching the ceiling, changing focus wildly, as if she were going mad. When next she spoke, her voice had the inflection and guttural gravity of a derelict.

"You *know* I *don't want* to do it."

"Do what?" I asked, terrified by her tone.

She seemed not to hear me and rolled her head from side to side, repeating, "You *know* I *don't want* to do it."

"For God's sake, Witte, what don't you want to do?"

"You *know* I *don't want* to do it." Each time she delivered the line in the same halting cadence, eyes skyward, scanning.

"Please," I pleaded, fearing she had a gun hidden under the cushion and was about to kill me. "Can't we talk this out?"

As I watched, frozen to the couch, Witte slowly rose and glided with regal composure into the bedroom. When she was out of sight, I heard her say again, "You *know* I *don't want* to do it."

I was frantic and lunged for our bedroom doorway. Witte began taking her clothes out of the closet and laying them on the bed. She packed a carton with Pattin's things from my desk. Her motions were deliberate and sure, but every once in a while she'd stop and repeat in a hoarse whisper to the ceiling that dreadful phrase, as if she was asking God for forgiveness.

When it finally dawned that she wasn't armed or about to attack but had decided to leave me, I braved another plea. "Okay, I'll stop seeing her. I'll find someone else, a male doctor of your choice. Please stop this silly packing."

Witte never missed a move. She completely ignored me and began putting my junk back in the drawers that she'd emptied. When she finished, she sidled past me to the phone and dialed her parents.

It was then about three in the afternoon. The snow had almost stopped. I could hear the plows grinding and scratching along Pine Street and the trumpeting of jubilant children having a snowball fight outside our window. Portland was coming back to life. Mine was about to end. I gravitated to the couch and tried not to listen.

"Hello, Daddy. Yes, we're fine, except for being snowed in. No, he's here. Portland Copper's closed. Is Mumma there? Yuh. Yuh, he's fine. She's good. Sleeps through, now. Awful good girl. Yuh.

"Huy Mumma. No, plant was closed. Mumma. Listen, Mumma. Karcher and I...We...We gotta separate for awhile.

"Please, Ma, let me finish. Yuh, but I need time to sort things out. No, figured Pattin and I'd come stay with you till things blow over. Mumma, I don't want to go into it now, on the phone. I know. I know. Okay, but can we come home? C...could Daddy pick us up tomorrow, when the roads are clear? Yuh. Nine o'clock? We'll be ready. Yuh. Mumma. *Ma*... We'll talk later. Thank Daddy. Bye."

During Witte's phone conversation I had been lying facing the backrest with a pillow over my ear, sniffing traces of her lavender powder that clung to the fabric. When she hung up I didn't move. It was really happening. I was being abandoned by a woman—again—and just as powerless to stop her exit.

But the situation wasn't hopeless, I tried to reassure myself. Witte had spoken to her mother about things blowing over, and I had Auburn to pull me through the separation. But not this week when I needed her most. My gut sank lower still.

Our last supper together was almost unbearable. Witte couldn't cook, and neither of us could eat. I heated some leftover slumgullion and fixed a honeymoon salad: lettuce alone. We sat in silence at opposite ends of the table, unable to pick up our forks.

In an attempt to banish the gloom I put on the radio. Through the evening skip, some Boston station was playing WW II oldies, including two that Witte and I had danced to on Saturday nights at the Varney Grange: "Born to Lose" and "I Wish I'd Never Seen Sunshine." They were standards in Loring's repertoire that had accompanied our courtship. Now their melancholy lilt so eloquently mirrored our predicament, we couldn't see our plates. We couldn't dance, but we let the music play, neither wishing to break the last band of love that bound us.

We lay together for the last time, locked in each other's arms. It never occurred to me to make love; it probably wouldn't have been possible anyway. I couldn't sleep so I gazed out the window. The snow curtained us from the street, but I could see the sky through the upper panes. Clouds were scudding past the sickle moon that hung over the tenements. It was my moon, the one I remembered outside my attic bedroom window as a child, hovering just above the trees at the far end of the field. Just a sliver, holding water. I took strength from my moon until it set and I fell asleep.

* * * * * * * *

Morning brought a bustle of activity that left no time for either of us to dwell on parting. Pattin was naturally upset by all the commotion and cried ceaselessly, especially hard when she saw her grandfather's face. I helped Witte as best I could. We piled everything in the hall in readiness, and not a moment too soon. Loring's loud thumping at the door was unmistakable. Witte let her father in. I tried to hide in the bathroom but was ordered out.

"Stickney. You in there?" Loring boomed at the door. "Y...yes, sir. Be right out."

I was reminded of the time I took too long in the tub at the Murch residence one Saturday before the dance and was ordered out in those same certain terms.

Loring was waiting to speak to me in the living room. He was pacing when I came in, rocking his head and masticating more than ever.

"Stickney, (smack, smack), you're a damn fool to let her go."

"I'm afraid she's determined, sir."

"Zat so? (smack, smack, pop) Look hear, Stickney." Loring draped a heavy arm around my shoulder and spoke close to my right ear. "Ever since Witte was a bud, she's been dogged as a midge. Now that she's flowered, wild horses can't drag her off course." Almost in a whisper, "If she's a mind to leave, and you let her go, she's stubborn enough to stay gone for good. You're taking an awful chance."

"What am I to do, tie her down?"

"If one of my cows took a fit to bein' skittery, d'you suppose the bull'd just stand there and let her run off?"

"Actually, I don't believe in force, sir. And I don't think you do either, or you wouldn't be here."

Loring clapped me on the back and bellowed, "I like you, Stickney. Always have." He picked up an armload of Witte's gear and headed for the door, calling over his shoulder, "You know where to find her." He waved and was gone.

Witte came out of the bedroom with Pattin in her arms. Her expression made me feel so guilty, I could hardly look at her. Not only was her mouth reduced to a dot, but her eyebrows were raked to an impossible angle. Her hair was severely drawn back, accentuating her tall, furrowed forehead and swan-length neck, which was bent forward in resignation. She kissed me tenderly on the forehead and croaked through choked tears, "I'm so sorry, dear."

Of our parting, I remember most the feel of Pattin's tiny, plush hand batting my cheek and the awful whine of Loring's truck going through the gears up Pine Street.

Chapter 12

MONA

After Witte left, the strangest feeling came over me as I paced the apartment, trying to sort the pieces to my life. I began talking to myself as I often did when alone, but this time I didn't recognize my voice. It was confident. What's more, I wasn't rolled up in a ball on the couch, crying. I felt no nausea, no jitters, no need to straighten everything in sight. It was as if I had installed a new self-steering gear.

"Okay, Karcher, get some clothes on. Call Dory and tell him you'll be in after lunch. Finish shoveling the sidewalk and dig out the Model A. Right. Into the shower."

There was no time to dwell on the past. I had commitments—to myself, to my job, to the city. With a fresh sense of who I was, I charged into my chores. The snow fairly flew from my shovel. I had the Ford unburied and running before lunch. Only once, when I heard the starter moan, did I wince, remembering the sound from Loring's truck departing.

Dory was sympathetic to my predicament and expressed optimism about Witte's return. "You'll learn that Maine women seldom hold a grudge," he said as I unlocked my desk. "Most get their feelings out quick, so they're open to change. If Witte sees you mend your ways, she'll come back. My wife did." I wasn't that confident, but I thanked him for his advice and buckled down to work.

On the way home, instead of being preoccupied with the dread of isolation, I found myself furious at Auburn for getting sick in my hour of need and for causing my rift with Witte. It was obvious I couldn't count on her support, let alone her love, which was fragmented and fickle. More important, I didn't need her anymore, or any other therapist for that matter. I was, amazingly, able to manage my own life. Why couldn't I have seen this clearly when Witte was still with me and quit Auburn in time?

Because I had to be alone to experience my strength, I answered myself. With Witte as my audience I could play the role of dependent and never have to call on my inner resources. So long as I made Witte a mouthpiece for Nettie, I remained a child in her presence. No longer able to hide behind Witte's or Auburn's skirts, I had to think and behave as a man.

I was so taken by my new status that I wanted to share it with others, especially anyone who could benefit from my instant wisdom. I scanned my memory for a new audience.

The first picture that came to mind was of Auburn's circle of clients incarcerated in the empty store room. Compared with any one of them, I was now a king of self-control. Perhaps I could help extricate one of them from Auburn's web as I had done.

It seemed so obviously the right thing to do, but it took me better than a week to get up the courage to do anything about it.

The following Thursday I took the risk. As soon as I got in the door I went straight to the phone book and looked up the one person I thought I could help most: Mona. Auburn had forbidden us to contact one another outside the group, but I happened to remember Mona's last name, Jaeger, because it was the same as a popular portable cement mixer's one-lunger, and I knew she was single and living in town. Her number was listed. She answered immediately, sounding timorous as ever, and almost hung up on me before I could explain my breakthrough.

"Mona, wait. Please. We're all in this life raft together. We've gotta help each other. We need to talk."

She agreed to meet me at Vi's for coffee at seven but only after she'd extracted a promise that I wouldn't breathe a word of our rendezvous to anyone, especially Auburn. I felt deliciously in control and decided to have supper at Vi's rather than wallow in Witte's kitchen. After my second shower of the day I put on a fresh pair of chinos and my heather sweater, splashed on some Mennen aftershave, and headed for Exchange Street. Arriving at Vi's at six-twenty, invigorated and ravenous, I had time to down a double cheeseburger, a plate of fries and a vanilla frappe before Mona arrived.

Just before seven I began looking out the window for her when I saw this waif wrapped in a huge wool shawl pass by. It was Mona but I couldn't tell for the enveloping raiment. A moment later she passed by again going the other way. This time when she took a furtive peek through the glass I recognized her asymmetrical smile. Rushing to the door, I caught up with her at the corner as she was about to turn down Fore Street. I knew she had decided not to meet me.

"Mona. Hi. I hardly recognized you in that wrap. It's been, what, almost eight months? How are you?"

"Petrified, Karcher. I shouldn't be here."

"No, really. It's okay. No one knows. Mona, I'm so glad to see you. Listen, c...can we get inside where it's warm? I'm freezing."

She looked even thinner than I remembered, and her sparse straw hair was scattered about her face, accentuating the wild look in her albino eyes. "You don't know what I've been through. It's horrific. I'm not sure I should be talking to you. Auburn said..."

"I know the rules, Mona, but this is a matter of survival, for both of us. Come and have some coffee."

"Okay, but just one cup. I get so jittery."

My confidence vanished as quickly as it had arrived. I couldn't believe I was offering emotional help to someone else. Me, the one who'd lost his wife, the one who woke nights in a cold sweat of panic anxiety, terrified he might vomit. The idea of assisting anyone with their problems seemed suddenly ludicrous. Apparently my discomposure showed as Mona was studying me with this pinched expression, her head listing to starboard.

"Karcher, are you *sure* you want to do this?"

"Oh, yes. Yes, of course." I forced a smile.

Shaking off my misgivings, I offered her my arm and headed back to Vi's place. We took a table in the corner furthest from the window and the counter and sat opposite one another. We both decided to have hot chocolate instead of coffee; it was more comforting, and it so loosened

Mona's tongue that we stayed over an hour and had several cups. I did most of the listening.

It seemed that Auburn had made a forceful pass at Mona during their weekly session early in January, leaving Mona terrified and tormented. She desperately loved Auburn in the confused way a preschool girl loves her mother. But Auburn knew Mona's weakness in sexual identity and exploited it to the fullest. When Mona reacted in horror, Auburn tried to shame her into believing she was a freak, which, in Mona's case, didn't take much convincing. The result: Mona had a nervous breakdown and landed herself in Maine Medical. She was just beginning to feel half human when I called; it couldn't have come at a better time.

"Mona," I said tentatively when she finished, "I know it's hard to believe, but this woman we love is dangerous. Remember Fred? Why do you think he committed suicide? Sure, he was disturbed, but Auburn put him over the edge, literally. Look at what's happened to me and Witte. And to you.

"If we give her half a chance, she'll finish us off, too. She's insatiable. I don't want to see you go down like that, and I think I can help."

"How? She's got the medical degree, not us. If we try and discredit her, who'll believe a couple of misfit psychos?"

"No. Don't you see? We don't have to discredit her, just stop seeing her, and try and convince the others to do the same. Without clients to feed on, she'll die."

"She'll just find other dupes like us to ravage."

"Not if we get the word out. Look, I have an idea. Why don't you and I form an alliance, a coalition for honesty in psychotherapy? Posters, picketing, sidewalk interviews, radio spots, rallies, the works. Bet the others would join us."

"You *are* mad, Karcher. But I have to admit, I like the idea. Do you think we'd get away with it, I mean, without getting arrested?"

"Who can arrest the truth? Besides, we have our first amendment rights.

"Seriously? Sure, we might be arrested for demonstrating, but that's nothing. I'm up for a night in the clink if necessary, to get that bitch. How about you?"

"I don't know. Sounds kinda risky. But I guess it's done all the time for other good causes. What the hell, it's worth a try."

Mona looked at her watch. "Karcher, I gotta go." She stood and shook my hand. "Thanks for listening. See yuh." She smiled and was gone.

On my walk home, I reflected on Mona's smile. It wasn't mysterious like her namesake's in da Vinci's portrait, but it was no less sincere.

Chapter 13

DANA STREET

Buoyed by the prospect of putting Auburn out of business, or at least making it difficult for her to attract new clients, I returned to 157b Pine, superficially oblivious of my desolation. Without thinking, I put on all the lights and cranked up WGAN loud enough to obliterate any memories that might bubble up and disturb my scheming. Pacing seemed the best stimulus for creative thinking. Truth is, I was too discomposed to sit.

Anger fired my imagination and focused my resources. My first priority was to break relations with this wanton woman who had the audacity to call herself my psychiatrist. That accomplished, and the sooner the better, I had to convince the others to do the same and band with Mona and me to discredit her. My motive, subconscious at the time, was to demonstrate loyalty to Witte in the hope of winning her back. My termination with Auburn had to be convincing.

It had to appear amicable: express joy at finding my inner strength through therapy, assure her that I felt strong enough now to go it alone, but request permission to recontact her should I regress, and thank her for turning my life around. It shouldn't be too hard to carry off, as one of my ambivalent selves believed much of it was true. One session should do it. Two at the most.

The hard part would be rallying support from the others. We needed an irresistible common motive, such as an unconscionable form of emotional abuse that we had all experienced, to pull the group together. That would take research, which presumed cooperation for interviews. Even if they all agreed to be questioned and spilled their guts, a cohesive picture of Auburn's subterfuge might not emerge. It was a long shot but one that had to be taken.

I went to the phone book and prepared a telephone list of Auburn's potential mutineers. Fred, God rest his soul, couldn't help us; I doubt he would have had the guts anyway. Douglas N. Bolter Jr. (Greer) was listed at 5 Bayberry Lane in Falmouth, and Rollag's Kennel had an indented listing under it in the Gorham section: Harry S. and Porcher M. Rollag, followed by the number. Auburn surely had other clients I hadn't met so I left room for several more names before writing "Goals and Procedures."

It was then almost midnight, and I was sufficiently unwound to hit the sack without fear my mind would drift back to Witte before I fell asleep. But I couldn't block my dreams.

Auburn and I were naked and writhing on her couch, locked in the full performance of passion, when the door to her sanctum flew open revealing Witte's backlighted silhouette holding a revolver trained on us. As we scrambled to cover ourselves, I heard that dreaded derelict's voice erupt from Witte's throat: "You *know* I *don't want* to do it."

I shouted, "No," just before the magnesium-white flash and deafening crack—and sat bolt upright in bed, wide awake and in a cold sweat.

The dream replayed again later that night and haunted me at random for more than a week. There was always only one shot, and invariably I'd wake before learning who got hit. I was afraid to go to sleep for fear the next time it would be resolved and the victim would be me.

I hoped that in time my righteous plan of retaliation would pacify Witte's ghost and put an end to the nightmare, but my plotting only seemed to perpetuate it. When sharing the fantasy with Mona failed to defuse it, I downed a couple of 8 mg Trilafon which Auburn had prescribed to quell my anxiety attacks. I slept undisturbed that night but paid for the intervention next morning with nonstop memories of Witte.

Auburn called on Friday evening as I was on my way out the door to meet Mona, saying that her fever had broken and that we should plan to meet the following Wednesday. Although somewhat nasal, her velvet voice so mesmerized me that I wanted to scrub my dastardly plot on the spot. I expressed pleasure at her convalescence and made no mention of termination.

Termination? Nothing was further from my mind. I started to tell her how much I'd missed her, but she cut me off, saying she had several other patients to call.

My insides were melting but I'd made a commitment to Mona and to myself. Furious at the conflict raging within my heart, I broke from the apartment for Mona's garret on a dead run without donning more than a sweater. Lucky for me the sidewalks had been sanded as I was pushing hard to shake out a solution before I arrived, not wanting to appear undecided after instigating Auburn's fall from grace.

Mona's condition left no doubt as to the right course of action. She didn't come to the door but called weakly for me to enter. I found her in a ball on the bare floor, crying, a half finished oil lamp bowl on the potter's wheel and the fire in the stove nearly out. When I bent to comfort her, she pushed me away.

"I'm no good with her, and I can't bear to be without her like this, Karcher. I just this minute got off the phone with her. Can you imagine, she called to try and convince me to come back?"

"I just got a call from her myself, not a half hour ago. Must be a full moon." I paused. Getting no reaction from Mona, I continued. "Strange as it may seem, I'm in the same quandary. Auburn's like heroin; once hooked, you can't kick the habit. Well, by God, we two are gonna kick her where it hurts and go on with our lives." I pounded the floor with my fist. "No person has the right to control us. Only we know what's right for ourselves. If there's one thing I've learned these last few days, it's this: We have within us the resources to survive—alone, if necessary. But it doesn't have to be one extreme or the other, an all-consuming relationship or desolation. We can have deep feelings for another person without giving up our autonomy. Each of us is invincible."

Mona uncoiled and gave me her hand. "Boy, you're right about that. Nobody's going to fuck up our lives unless we're stupid enough to let them." She drew a ragged breath. "Why then do I miss her so?"

"Because she's such a convincing surrogate mother, and you and I, having missed our mothering when we needed it most, are vulnerable. The problem is not with our needs but with Auburn's insincerity. She's just acting but we believe she means it. Goddamn woman should be on the stage."

"Okay, so who do we turn to now, to fill our mothers' shoes?"

"No one. We take care of ourselves. Remember me saying that we have all the ingredients within us to carry on? Well, that includes mothering. I think each of us has inside them many persons, some male, some female. Some may take on form and shape from time to time, and talk to us like a parent, a sibling, a peer—scolding us, reassuring us, loving us. When we open ourselves to receive these inner voices, we become strong. Our chin rises, we swagger and we smile. The world around us is no longer a threat because we are whole."

"Jeezus, Karcher. You sound like a psychologist. Where'd you learn all that stuff?"

Mona was up and rekindling the fire. The spark of curiosity had returned to her face, and her body moved with confidence, scuttling the ashes, stoking and adjusting the draft. I was relieved, almost proud to have transformed her mood.

"Believe it or not, I learned some of it from Auburn. But it never stuck until I put it to the test, when Witte left me. When I found myself suddenly alone in our apartment, the voices were too loud to ignore. I couldn't feel sorry for myself anymore. My audience was gone."

"That's super, Karcher. With that compass of yours, you'll be so securely on track, you'll have to fight Witte off with a club." She gave me a wink on the way to the kitchen. "How about some coffee?"

"Sure, thanks. Black and bitter."

"Mister Tough Guy." She chuckled. "You know, Karcher, your philosophy's beginning to rub off on me."

"Good, then we can get started."

* * * * * * * *

It occurred to me on the way home that it really didn't matter whether we beat Auburn down or not so long as we were free. Extrication never looked so feasible. Mona didn't even have to weather another session; she'd been clean of the substance Auburn for months. I on the other hand had to endure another fifty minutes of the consummate actress.

Wednesday took forever to come, and my inner voices had to work overtime, shouting themselves hoarse to keep my defenses elevated. I think my recurring nightmare was primarily responsible for keeping me on track, relentlessly reminding me of my infidelity. It was logical to assume that once I dismissed Auburn, the dream would vanish. Atonement, however, took much longer than I expected.

Auburn greeted me at her office door wearing a loosely secured dusty rose bathrobe which barely concealed her enormous assets. "How's my favorite knight, tonight?" she purred in that devastating, smoky contralto, her arms open wide to receive me. The heat and musk radiating from her sumptuous body sucked me into her embrace before I could resist.

"Uhhh," I groaned, enjoying her inertia. "Substantial Queen, I feel fine, all things considered. And you?"

Auburn locked the door and edged our bodies toward the couch. "I'm better than all better, Karcher. But what did you mean by 'all things considered'?"

"Well, a lot has happened in the last two weeks, some good, some not so good. Witte left me a week ago for her folks. Without warning she started packing Sunday afternoon, the day of the big storm. Next morning she was gone. I thought I was going to kill myself right there on the doorstep, but a moment later I felt completely in control, and I've been in control ever since except for being haunted by a recurring dream."

"Congratulations, Karcher."

"Yup, I think I've finally kicked my insecurity, thanks to you."

"No—thanks to Karcher. *You* did it; not I. Sometimes it takes a shock to jolt the self-correcting forces within us into action. See how strong your resources are? I knew you had it in you all along." She poked at my solar plexus. "I think this calls for a celebration." She started to tip me back on the couch.

"Auburn, I..."

"R-e-l-a-x, Karcher."

By this time I was horizontal. Auburn was astride my waist and beginning to untie her robe. My confused heart pounded irregularly. After so long without a woman's touch I was hungry for release, and a part of me—more than I cared to admit—was still in love with Auburn. But I couldn't let this happen.

"Listen, Auburn. There's more." I struggled to right myself.

"Can't it wait, Karcher? I need you. I've waited almost two years for this." The bodice of her robe had fluttered to my thighs, and I was no longer in full control of the lower half of my body. With fists clenched I forced myself to a seated position and hugged her, trying to erase the image of her huge mammaries and inviting lips hovering inches above my nose.

"I...I'm just not up for this."

"You feel up to it to me, and that's more than we can say of previous encounters, sweetheart."

"Look," I said, wriggling under her steamy mass, "I'm doing so well now that I figured I'd try going it alone, if that's okay with you."

Auburn slid back to clear my fly. Her breathing had become labored and her eyes burned with desire. She gestured in the direction of my zipper. "Be my guest."

"Auburn, you're not listening to me. I think we ought to terminate." I paused. When I saw her eyes narrow, I knew I'd gotten her attention.

"WHAT?"

"This is very hard for me, too, but I think it's best. I'm finally feeling comfortable enough to hack it on my own, without a woman if need be. It's important that I maintain that independence."

"Independence doesn't mean you have to be celibate, Karcher. You're a sensitive and sexy guy. Witte may not appreciate that, but I do."

"Witte left a wimp. Now that I've become a man, she'll return. You'll see."

"If you're so sure of your masculinity, Karcher, why can't you make love to me?"

"Because—*finally*—I know who I am. I know what I want, and I'll be God damned if I'll let you fuck up my chances for a reunion. Is that clear?"

"Yes, sir!"

Auburn saluted me with comic excess. I could see that my outburst had just added fuel to her fire. I was going to have to get ugly.

"You think this is just a game of chess and I'm one of your pawns to toy with, like the others. Well, I'm sick of it. I don't want to have sex with you. I just want to get out of here and get on with my life."

"No big deal, Karcher honey. If you want to talk, we'll talk. Shoot." Auburn slid to the edge of the couch and pulled her robe high around her neck, struck a saucy pose and pretended to be all ears.

"Auburn, I've learned a lot in our sessions: to be proud to be a man, self-sufficient and less blown by the winds of society; to come to better terms with my mother; and to cherish my relationship with Witte—too late, perhaps, and there's the rub.

"I got hooked on you. Instead of keeping your distance, you took advantage of my vulnerability to satisfy your insatiable need to be loved. So instead of transferring my love to Witte, I resented her. You orchestrated our separation."

"Wrong, Karcher. You brought it on by being insecure and dependent as a child. You said so yourself. No woman wants that in a man."

"But she could also see I was in love with you."

"Well, are you?"

"See, you're so hung up on receiving your so-called Universal Love, you can't see my predicament. It's not enough just to become secure. I've got to stop seeing you to win her back. Even that may not be enough."

"What do you mean, 'not enough'?"

I wanted to taunt her by saying "Worried?" but kept my cool.

"I mean, it's going to take a lot of convincing to turn Witte around. She didn't take her stand lightly."

"The problem with people like Witte—and I love her dearly, Karcher, as well you know—is that they can't see beyond the facts. Life for them is black or white. Subtle shadings, transitory emotions, ephemeral experiences— things you and I understand—pass them by. Witte's kind can't grasp concepts like Universal Love; they can only handle being in love with one person at a time. Such tunnel vision denies them life's full measure of richness. It's tragic."

"Sorry to disappoint you, Queenie, but I too fall into your condemned-to-love-one-at-a-time category. Having to make a choice between lovers has been tearing my heart apart. If only I could embrace your concept. Guess my heart just isn't big enough."

"Gee, and here I'd figured you for a bacchanal Henry VIII."

"Whoops. That puts you in jeopardy, as one of my promiscuous queens. Hmmmm."

"Don't get morbid, Karcher."

"*Your* analogy, Auburn."

"The point is, you don't have to choose between Witte and me. Why limit your perspective? Enrich yourself. You deserve it."

"It's very seductive. Probably every man's dream. But look around you. How many others do you see comfortably juggling two romances, let alone three, or six? I consider myself among the vast majority who'd fumble, and that doesn't make me dull and boring. Commitment isn't a sin, Auburn."

"Certainly not. I'm committed to *all* those I love. I give each of my special clients a different facet of myself, and they return a unique part of themselves to me. Harry is my guardian and indefatigable lover. Fred, poor darling, used to write me love poems and read them here in the dark so I couldn't see him crying. Porcher loves to wrestle with me in the nude; I know that sounds kinky, but it's her special way of sharing. Mona always brings me a pastry, candy or tort that she's baked especially for our visit. She sits on my lap and we feed each other. Greer brings her oils and easel, and I pose in the buff for her while we listen to Mozart. Dear Doug takes voice and breathing lessons from me; he always has me put on a tight powder blue sweater. And I never tire of lying in your arms, feeling the stroke of your incredibly sensitive hands and listening to you talk. You see, I love you all."

"You didn't mention your husband, Basil."

"Basil gives me stability, moral support, a place to come home to. He always lends a sympathetic ear. Cooks a mean brunch, too. No, I couldn't do what I do without big Basil's grounding."

"Sure convenient having a cuckold in a business like yours."

"Basil understands my needs perfectly. He's not naive. He has his own life and knows not to interfere in mine."

"No wonder his eyes keep closing involuntarily. He can't bear to watch what's going on."

"You just can't conceive of two people living together with space between them, can you, Karcher? Too much exposure can crush a marriage. If people make constant demands on one another, love dies. 'Live and let live' is the motto I subscribe to."

"You've got it all figured, haven't you? You're as bad as Nettie. No, you're worse. Tell me, are you happy? Really? I want to know."

"Yes, I am, Karcher, hard as that may be for you to fathom. I'm doing what I love to do. My clients love and respect me. I make an adequate living. I have a devoted husband and three great kids. What more could a woman want?"

"Well, this is one client who's no longer enchanted by your operation. And I wouldn't be surprised to see others defect when they realize how they're being used. This is definitely the last time I pay for your abuse, but I rather suspect it won't be the last time I see you."

Undaunted, Auburn parried my jab with a big smile. "I hope not, 'cause there's a place in Queenie's heart that only Karcher can fill. This I promise: you'll always know where I am."

I was on my feet and moving.

"Good luck with that feisty gal of yours, Karcher."

I was now half way out the door, but Auburn opened her arms for one last hug. Reluctantly I turned back and drew her to me. Like a condemned prisoner silently pleading for mercy, she held on with "ardulustic" tenacity for almost a minute before letting me go. It was then that I realized Witte's bullet was intended for Auburn and not for me.

Chapter 14

NO SON

Although my final session with Auburn had not gone amicably as planned, it was over. I was relieved and more than a little proud at having pulled it off and wanted to spill the good news to Witte. But fearing rejection, I called Mona instead. As I unfolded the details of our confrontation, Mona's cheerful encouragement gradually faded to a whispered warning: "She's on to you, Karcher. Be careful."

"You may be right," I replied. "Maybe we should wait a while before contacting the others."

Mona suggested we meet again in May, still early enough to plan a summer demonstration. I stressed we needed more lead time to woo the group into our camp, but Mona insisted on a three month cooling off period to insure that Auburn would not associate our plot with my termination, should one of the group not go along with us and blow the whistle. We agreed to meet over Memorial Day weekend in Mona's tandem shell on Back Cove, weather permitting.

* * * * * * * *

Mud season in 1962 lasted from early March for a full month, perpetuated by spring rains as relentless as the recent snows. In the span of just three days Portland turned from dirty white to chocolate. The downhill streets ran like sewers to the sea. Few ventured forth, and when they did, they hunched under huge, black umbrellas and lunged from door to door. I, like most, stayed inside, preferring to press my nose to the kitchen pane and watch the rain pool and eddy before the drain. It was hard to revel in the season's change.

My first contact with the Murch family since Witte left came at five past six on a Thursday evening in early April. Loring called to complain that both his tractors and the D6 Caterpillar dozer were mired up to their axles. Could I come over on Saturday and give him a hand? Not a word about Witte or our separation. He spoke as if I was his long-time hired hand living just down the road whom he called upon regularly once or twice a week. It was difficult to conceal my excitement.

"S...sure. I'd be glad to, sir. That is, if it's okay with the others." I couldn't say Witte.

"Stickney," he bellowed into the phone, "*I* buried the bastards. Women had no part in it. Be here at seven."

"Yes, sir."

I put down the receiver and roared to release the tension I'd stored for more than a month, waiting for any sign of acceptance from Witte. Fearing almost certain rejection, I'd resisted telephoning, and after two weeks of no call or letter from her I knew I'd made the right decision. Since I'd settled into a pattern of acceptance, Loring's call caught me by surprise.

Knowing Loring, it was likely that the women hadn't even been notified, let alone consulted, about my visit.

Witte might be very surprised to see me. My insides curled with clandestine pleasure at the thought. All my systems locked in synchronous focus on her.

My activities for the next thirty-six hours were not recorded, but my body somehow managed to get fed and rested and make its expected appearance at work on Friday. On Saturday morning my brain came alive at five with schizophrenic indecision. Tormented about what to wear and no longer able to sleep, I headed for the shower. My oldest dungarees, wool socks and work boots, obviously, said the left side of my brain. Navy turtleneck, pressed chinos and white bucks, retorted the right. I prolonged my shower, hoping that the warm water on my head would melt the two halves and result in a harmonious resolution that would please both Witte and her father. Then I gave up and made the sensible choice.

The scene that greeted me at the Murch farm confirmed my decision to dress down. Loring had planked the path from the dooryard to the kitchen with four-quarter green pine to enable passage without sinking or tracking the brown ooze inside. Beside the powerhouse I could just see the canted yellow fuel tank seat of the Caterpillar dozer and the tip of its tall stack poking from the quagmire. Farther afield the upper half of Loring's John Deere tractor loomed, listing severely to port. Behind the barn lay the Farmall's pitiful red hulk, its nose to the sky. The Murch AA Ford truck was nowhere in sight.

The rain had stopped but the sky still seethed in sepia before the gull gray morning. I parked in the middle of the gravel driveway, the only hard ground, then picked my way along the planks to the back door and knocked. My heart was pounding terribly, and my hands were visibly shaking. I can only imagine the expression on my face when the door was opened by Loring. His head was already rocking.

"Come in, Stickney (smack, smack) Glad you're here. Doak'll be right along. I got us in a peck of trouble out there. Couldn't quit. You know me: Too damn stubborn."

I looked past him at the neat kitchen. Breakfast was all cleaned up. The wash kettle was upended and drying on the range rack. Only the coffee pot remained at a simmer on the back burner. The women were nowhere in sight.

"Coffee, Stickney?"

"Yes, thanks. Black is fine. Say, where are the women?"

"Just left for Witte's practice and to get groceries. Be gone most of the day, I 'spect."

My heart sank to my boots. "You mean they didn't know I was coming?"

"Oh, they knew all right. Witte, she's still kinda tender. Needs more time, Karcher." He dropped a heavy hand on my shoulder. "Now, don't get down in the mouth, boy. She'll come around."

"Practice? You said Witte was at practice? For what?"

"Twirlin'. Used to be good at it in school."

"I'll be darned. She never told me."

"Well, it's been a long time. She just decided to spruce up. Something to do, you know."

I heard a faint bump at the door and looked up to see Doak Durgin's hollow stare framed in the screened window. The sight of him made me mist up. Not since our wedding had I gazed into those sunken, yellowed eyes focused at infinity. It had been five years since he'd lost his daughter, Donna, because he'd failed to install lightning arresters on the peak of his house. Now, living alone in a trailer, his wife having left him after the fire, Doak slatted through what was left of his life like the blown out sail of an abandoned catboat, wearing his mistake indelibly on all quarters.

"Don't be bashful, Doak. Come on in," Loring shouted. The door slowly creaked open, and Doak eased his hulking form to the nearest chair where a mug of sweet, blonde coffee awaited him. He didn't say anything at first, just nodded to each of us and began sipping. The left breast pocket of his checkered wool shirt still bore the creases outlining Donna's picture, which he wore over his heart. I prayed that he wouldn't show it to me again and make me break down in front of Loring.

Much to my relief, Doak addressed the subject at hand. "Worked some to sink that Cat, Loring."

"Tweren't hard in that soup. Tugged at the Deere with her. Couple churns and she was under."

Loring rose to his full six feet and led us back through the laundry, the woodshed and the tractor stalls to the powerhouse. An unsteady breeze was rattling the rolling door behind the Klein, modulating the light that crept in through the cracks. Loring put on the light and unbarred the latch. Together we forced the door aside, fighting the rusty wheels along the overhead track. The scene outside was no less messy from my new perspective, but it seemed far from hopeless.

"The dozer's lined up pretty well with the Klein," I
noted. "How about we reel it in with a few turns of that
hawser around the crankshaft extension?" I gestured to a
coil of inch-and-a-half manilla in the corner by the door.

Loring shook his head. "Keyway'll gnaw that rope in
two quicker than a barn owl can gulp a vole."

"Maybe so," I said, "but by then the Cat'll be out of the
hole. And there'll still be enough length left to reach the
Deere."

"Got it all figured, have you, Stickney?"

I let Loring's remark pass, knowing how embarrassed
he was, and looked to Doak for support. He was sitting on
an overturned pail in the doorway, chewing his cud and
gazing out at the Farmall. Doak knew enough not to take
sides. Nodding in the direction of the second tractor, he
asked, "How you fixing to get her?"

Loring didn't wait for me to offer more advice. "She'll sit
right there till the ground firms up. Don't need her for a
while yet." He looked over at me and shook his finger. "I
know your angle, Stickney." Then he turned and
disappeared behind the Klein.

I heard the hiss of propane filling the accumulator and
knew he'd decided to try my idea. A moment later Loring
stepped from behind the engine's boiler-sized single
horizontal cylinder and hollered to me: "Climb them
spokes, boy."

My heart skipped several beats as I advanced on the
nearest of the Klein's two seventy-eight inch flywheels. I'd
helped crank the monster only once, four years before,
when the power went out on Thanksgiving during my first

visit to the farm. Loring had put me and Witte right to work. We men had cranked while Witte had tended the mixture.

"You take the left wheel, Doak, and mind the belt; lacing'll do an awful job on a man who isn't careful."

Orders given, Loring banged the brass petcock open. Doak and I began pulling her through. Looking down from my perch on the flywheel, instead of Loring's firm fists attacking the mixing valve I envisioned Witte's exquisite hands manipulating the petcock, deftly nudging the handle with her right palm while braking it with her left, as she had done when last I climbed those formidable spokes. She'd muffed the mixture on her first try, producing a weak false fire, but got it right the second time.

Perhaps it was the warmer weather, but I expect it was Loring's practiced touch that lit the beast on the second turn. I felt the spoke I clung to give way like a giant willow bow breaking slowly under my weight and found myself summarily deposited on the concrete foundation. The Klein's first fire forced a smoke star from the manifold flange just before the piston emerged from the open cylinder's black maw. I felt the explosion through my feet and followed the hollow boom as it rose in the chimney. The flywheels rolled lazily through the piston's remaining three strokes then lurched decisively as she hit the second time. I stepped back to clear the accelerating wheel and watched Loring fine tune the mixture, thrilling to the Klein's thunderous response: the building cadence of thuds, the roiling haze redolent with sulfur that rapidly permeated the powerhouse, the separated seismic tremors underfoot.

When the Klein had settled down and began producing a procession of tuba grunts, we uncoiled the hawser and lined it up with the Cat. Doak worked silently alongside us, cuing his movements to the inclination of Loring's bushy eyebrows. I soon fell into the rhythm and found myself quietly reveling in the efficiency of tacit teamwork.

Despite the crawler's nose-down attitude, its pony twin did not flood but burst into a staccato crackle at the first nudge of the starter. A few moments later Loring had the big Cat spewing a narrow funnel of diesel smoke and ringing its mournful note across the valley. We laid a grid of oak timbers behind the tracks and Loring climbed aboard. Doak tailed the hawser while I wound a few turns on the Klein's lazily spinning crankshaft. Slack taken, I tensioned the bite. The Klein's exhaust note hardened, smoke curled from the manilla coils, the Cat growled, but Doak only got a couple of inches, mostly stretch. I signaled Loring to try again. This time the dozer budged. It just got a purchase on the first timber when the hawser snapped at the hitch. Loring locked the tracks and held his ground. We spliced the rope and tried again. This time Doak got a good handful, and the Cat lurched up on the grid before the hawser burned through. Loring kept it going. Now floating on the oak, the big Cat ground steadily for the powerhouse, looming ever larger in the opening until it put out the light from the sky. With the dozer secure on the apron, Loring closed the fuel rack, and the Cat decrescendoed to its characteristic, gravelly lope, its weighted rain cap flapping just above the stack.

Loring was grinning, a rare occurrence. He climbed down and clapped me on the back. "Stickney," he roared, "you ain't half bad."

Doak sank to the overturned bucket and wiped his brow with his sleeve. "Damn lucky," he muttered, gazing at the smoldering stub of the hawser and the almost submerged lattice of timbers, several of which were shattered and poking their jagged shards skyward. "Damn lucky, that's all."

As it was nearly noon, Loring suggested we break for lunch. He shut down the Klein but left the Cat idling. "Girls fixed sandwiches," he noted on the way to the kitchen. At the door I squinted south along the road, hoping to see the tipsy silhouette of the Murch truck rounding the bend, trailing its tin pot rattle, but all I could see stirring down Broad Turn was a crow picking at an opossum carcass.

"Comin', Stickney?" Loring was leaning out the door with a chicken salad sandwich already in hand. He took a bite and masticated noisily. "Awful good," he added, after pushing the sandwich into his cheek.

I took my place at the kitchen table and stared at the diagonally cut sandwich with its crusts neatly excised. My mind reeled images of Witte. I watched her tapered, moonstone-tipped fingers paring the bread slices, smoothing the spread, patting together the layers, holding them just so and cutting on the bias with a quick rocking motion. Her head was tipped on one side to keep her hair out of her eyes as she worked. Her brow was knitted, full of concentration. Now she looked up to check on Pattin, who was trundling unsteadily past the stove, sucking her thumb while clutching a remnant of her mother's old bathrobe. She smiled, shook her head and bent to wrap my sandwich in waxed paper.

"Not hungry, Karcher?" Doak had already wolfed his sandwich and was slurping at his coffee.

"Uh...n...no, I was just daydreaming." I took a bite and looked out the window so they wouldn't see my eyes.

"Women," Doak lamented. "Can't live with 'em. Can't live without 'em. I don't know. I *just don't know*."

It was the cadence of Doak's comment more than what he said that finished me. I could smell the fading Russia Leather and wood smoke in Witte's hair, feel the cool, slippery rayon hugging her body, and hear her labored breathing and hoarse whispers behind the kitchen door. Without thinking I turned on my tormentor and brought my fist down hard on the oil cloth.

"Okay. Yeh, I miss her, Doak. Terribly. Makes me sick to think she had to knee me in the nuts and go, to teach me how much I love her. What a chump I am."

"She do that to you?" Loring was suddenly standing, leaning over the table, waving his index finger in my direction. The anguish in his squint spoke louder than his words and made his head rocking and masticating superfluous.

"Just a figure of speech," I answered quickly.

"Damn it, Stickney. Witte get 'cha below the belt?" He gripped both my shoulders and shook out the truth.

"Well...once, when I really aggravated her. I was being a real bastard."

"You take advantage of her, boy?" His lower lip drew up tight.

"No, sir. I'd never force a woman. I was just sassing her."

Loring slid his hands from my shoulders to my forearms and bent closer. I could smell the coffee on his breath and the diesel fuel on his sleeve. "My fault, son." His rheumy eyes were unavoidable. "Taught her that when she was just a zephyr, so's she'd be able to defend herself." He squinted and pumped my arms a little. "Look, a filly built like Witte—well—she'd have to shut a fella down quick." He shook his head. "I'm awful sorry, Karcher."

"I deserved it, sir."

Doak, who had been taking this all in, turned his chair toward me and summed up the situation. "Least your wife gave you a warning." When his mouth closed, the corners turned down and the hollow returned to his cheeks. He placed his hand to his breast pocket. "Donna, she never had a chance to defend herself."

I changed the subject quickly, suggesting we get back to work. Loring looked relieved and began to clear the table. I joined him, but Doak just sat there staring out the window.

"Pinin' won't get that tractor up," Loring observed as he slid the last plate into the sink and led us two lumpers back through the ell to the powerhouse. "Trouble with men is, they worry too much about women."

Loring sidelined the Cat on the apron to clear the tow path to the John Deere while I long-spliced the hawser once more and hitched it to the tractor. Then we fired up the Klein.

Although the alignment was poor, the Klein jerked the spidery tractor from its slough in one tug, nearly toppling Loring in the process. Only his bronco-breaking acrobatics saved him. Doak and I quickly reeled in the tippy green twin with its flailing passenger before the ooze reclaimed them. I was in stitches, watching my dignified father-in-law marionette struggling to maintain his equilibrium at the end of my string.

Loring, understandably, was not amused. "Stickney," he hollered over the Deere's staccato sputter when both man and machine were securely grounded on the apron, "Witte was right on the mark." He pushed in the Deere's magneto ground then climbed down and closed the Klein's petcock, opened its switch and waited for the rumpus to subside before continuing. His tone was clipped as he burned me with his daughter's unflinching glare. "Your idea of a joke, boy?"

"N...no, sir."

"What was it then, you had on your pea-sized brain, to do a thing like that?"

"I was just doing what we planned, to get the tractor unstuck."

"We?"

"It seemed like the only practical way, and it worked."

"Ayuh. And I suppose you think that justifies risking a mud bath for the jockey, or worse. I could have broken my damn neck."

"I guess I didn't think about the consequences."

"Stickney, if *ever* I'm fool enough to ask for your help again, be sure to kick me in the ass." He broke his stare, turned and slipped behind the Klein to shut off the gas. I looked around for Doak, but he was nowhere in sight. In a feeble attempt to quell my anxiety, I began coiling the remains of the hawser. Loring reappeared and started rolling closed the huge, hanging door. Once more its rusty iron wheels creaked and rumbled.

"Aren't you going to cover the tractor and dozer?" I asked timidly.

Loring didn't answer but kept the door rolling, shutting my Andrew Wyeth scene to a slit until, with a resounding boom, the powerhouse reverted to its former dingy state, lighted only by the single twenty-five watt bulb that hung from its cord over the Klein. I heard the clump of Loring's heavy boots receding through the woodshed on his way back to the kitchen. A moment later the light went out, and I was left alone in the shadows with my giant iron friend.

It didn't take much reflection to conclude that I'd taken a terrible risk, not only with Loring's physical well-being but with his allegiance. He alone in the Murch family had withheld judgment and kept in touch. I respected that.

Without Loring's support I knew I stood little chance of reclaiming Witte. Not that she took any cues from her father; Witte was autonomous. It was I who needed the stable platform on which to stand to sell the reconciliation. And it was I who had, figuratively speaking, stepped into the mud.

There was no time to lose. I had to patch things up before the girls came home. I moved toward a crack of daylight in the door and looked at my watch. Three o'clock. Witte could return at any moment. I found the inside passage and felt my way along the cords of split oak in the woodshed, lurched across the empty Farmall stall, tripped over the Maytag's oily exhaust hose that snaked across the laundry floor, and regained my balance just in time to avoid crashing into the closed kitchen door.

While I stood there working up the courage to confront Loring, I heard the brittle bounce of "The Johnson Rag" coming from the old Sterling upright in the parlor. I recognized immediately Loring's style: the flowery treble figures and urgent downbeats that drove us all to dance. He was playing to dissolve his troubles—vexations that failed to succumb to his masticating and head rocking. I knew that music therapy worked for him and decided to postpone my entrance until he'd completed the two step, one of the more energetic numbers in his repertoire.

When he began "God's Little Candles," I felt it safe to go in. The kitchen was as we had left it, neat and empty, but scented with wood smoke and spiced apples from Ida's overflowing pies. I tiptoed past the pantry into the parlor and seated myself in the love seat at Loring's back. Doak was crouched by the window, sniffling and staring across the valley. Neither acknowledged my presence.

I thought of putting on some coffee but couldn't take my eyes off of Loring's long fingers fluttering over the keys. They worked with such delicate dexterity, I couldn't believe they belonged to a working man. When he finished the waltz he spun around on the stool to address me. His voice was calm and philosophical, almost kindly.

"Stickney, you and I got off to a bad start today. I don't want that to spoil our friendship." I sighed with relief.

Loring squinted in preparation for the hard part. "Now, listen close." I braced myself with a quick breath.

"I never had a son, Karcher. Ida, she couldn't have any more children. Well, when you came sniffin' after Witte, I said to my wife, 'Maybe God didn't forget us after all,' and she wept. She prayed that you'd be our son. That's why it rankles me so when you act like that." He blinked—just once—and changed the subject.

"Life is never easy, Stickney. You're young yet, full of ideas. In time you'll learn that things go better when you pull steady instead of bullin'.

"Now, you better go before the women find you here." He stood, and I rose and moved to the door. I wanted to hug him but offered my hand instead. He gripped it firmly and flashed a deep vee smile. "Patience, Karcher. Patience, that's all."

I waved to Doak as I passed the window, but he looked right through me. Compared to his burden, my predicament seemed a mere trifle. But back in the Model A I cried for both of us.

I'd gone less than a mile when the Murch Ford express hove into view, wobbling toward me. I leaned long and hard on the klaxon and waved frantically. The truck driver lifted a small and tapered index finger from the wheel. Through my tears I saw Loring's disappointed eyes and knew I had a while yet to wait.

Chapter 15

FIGUREHEAD

Humiliated as I was, I couldn't ignore the umbilical tickle and weak kneed signature of hope. Witte's eyes behind the flivver's quivering plate glass windshield had set my tape loop rolling again, reminding my gut that I'd failed her. But this time it wasn't listening; my insides were rejoicing. I was a member of the Murch family, for better or for worse. Loring's acceptance made all the difference.

Ironically, I was beginning to enjoy the separation. Although Witte had certainly given me no encouragement, Loring's faith in me made the prospect of a reunion a certainty in my mind. I felt as if I was fasting with full knowledge that a baked Alaska was waiting for me in the not too distant future. Not knowing just when the feast was scheduled made the waiting all the more exciting.

The skies finally cleared the first week in May and Portland burst into bloom. With the rising thermometer came a building restlessness that peaked my anticipation. In my distracted, euphoric state, I completely forgot about my upcoming date, rowing with Mona in her shell; so that when the phone rang late on Sunday evening and I heard a woman's voice say, "Karcher, you still want to share some pulling?" I blurted, "Witte?"

"Blond, raggy, pectoral, with dirty fingernails."

"Oh, boy. I am a wreck. Mona, forgive me. Solitary confinement does things to a man's mind. Sure, I'd love to part the waters with you. Sunday before Memorial Day, right?"

"You're on. My place at ten."

Discrediting Auburn was the furthest thing from my mind. I hoped that Mona and I could enjoy the exercise, if not in silence, then without discussing our unpleasant past. But between the two of us, Mona was the one likely to remain alone. She had little to lose by alienating the others, and I knew the subject would come up.

WGAN's weather prognosis for the Memorial Day weekend was ideal: afternoon temperatures reaching seventy, a light southerly breeze and no precipitation. I spent Saturday at the curb on Commercial Street, servicing my Ford, taking breaks to watch the gulls swoop and squawk over the draggers' nets. Among the city and sea folk bustling about the waterfront I saw an occasional young woman traipsing the cobblestones along Fisherman's Wharf on her way to and from Morong's Fish Market. I strained to find in one that poignant resolve, that focused intensity, but none had the thrust, the sway, the confident carriage of the one I longed for.

I harbored this crazy idea that, in the event Witte found herself unable to forgive me, her double would turn up on the street. We'd meet, fall in love and resume without discontinuity the life Witte and I had had before the separation, as if nothing had changed. It was my defense against the worst case scenario.

The longer Witte and I remained out of contact, the more intense became my obsession to find a replacement. In vain the search continued, usually over a plate of beans at Vi's, and later, as I prowled Portland's entertainment district until I grew too weary and despondent to go on. Back at the empty apartment I'd go through an entire box of Kleenex while listening to heartbreaking ballads drifting uncertainly through the night from WWVA.

But while my disturbed mind was capable of conjuring Witte's clone, it couldn't cope with replicating Pattin's miniature deep vee Murch smile, to say nothing of finding a surrogate father half as fine as Loring. I had no choice. The real Witte had to be won. And that meant Auburn had to be discredited, even if Mona and I had to do the job alone.

* * * * * * * *

Sunday dawned cool and misty, promising more good weather for our row. I felt unusual concern for my hygiene that morning and topped off a thorough scrubbing with powder. Selecting a pair of white shorts that Witte had bleached for special summer occasions, matching socks and a striped polo shirt, I looked ready for rugby but reeked like a lilac bush in bloom.

The preening was wasted on Mona, who greeted me at the door in a sweat suit with, "Jeez, you're going to freeze your butt off." She urged me inside and immediately began rummaging behind the door for something to cover my exposed flesh, which I felt suddenly embarrassed revealing. "Here, I think these'll fit you." She handed me a rank pink pair of sweat pants, apparently the lower half of her backup suit, which I obligingly donned with difficulty. They barely reached my socks. Mona chuckled. "You may wish you'd brought a sweater, Karcher."

"I'll be fine, Mona. Really. Thanks."

"You like trail mix?" She held up a plastic bag brimming with various seeds, peanut hearts, raisins, and God knows what else.

"Is that lunch?" I asked meekly.

"Yup, along with yogurt and cider."

I swallowed hard before answering. "Guess you know what you're doing."

Mona pulled a red terry sweat band over her head and pointed to the oars racked on the wall. "The boat's already strapped down on my Beetle. We'll tie the sweeps to the rack on either side." She grabbed our grub and held the door for me to snake through the two pair of nine foot spruce spoons. Her car occupied one stall of a dilapidated garage two blocks away. Atop the red oxide VW was this plywood splinter—you couldn't call it a boat. The thing overhung the car on either end by three feet. Nearly slab-sided and with a beam of barely two feet, it didn't take much figuring to assess the craft's stability. As if its shape wasn't sufficiently convincing, Mona had affixed a small, carved cherub to the bow to appease Father Neptune.

"You've got to be kidding, Mona."

"Made her myself. She goes like stink with two."

I noted the flat bottom and decking, the crude coaming, the fingernail polish pink paint. "Uh-huh, I can just imagine. How much beer did it take to get your first mate aboard?"

"Nothing to it. You'll see."

"I wouldn't miss this for the world."

Mona carefully threaded the shell through Portland traffic and out along Baxter Boulevard to the launch site. We rigged the boat on a sliver of beach and skidded it into a full tide. I was instructed to brace an oar athwartship behind me, with the grip in the sand, before transferring my weight to the sliding seat. This she demonstrated with practiced agility, hardly disturbing Back Cove's glassy surface.

"Your turn. Remember, clamp the coaming then move your ass low and slow."

I laid the oar, scrunched down, got a good grip, swung aboard—and over I went. The water was only a few inches deep so I got more humiliated than wet. Mona thoughtfully suppressed her laughter and helped me right the boat. "You're supposed to put more oar on shore than to sea, klutz. Now, try again."

My second attempt was ultimately successful, but the boat shivered awfully in the process, sending out a succession of ripples to announce my incompetence to the others using the cove.

Once seated at an uneasy equilibrium, Mona showed me how to balance the boat using the oars as outriggers, grips clenched, spoons up. When she attempted to careen the boat to illustrate its augmented stability, to my surprise it stayed upright. "OK, hold your brace while I come aboard."

Mona swooped to the bow seat behind me, and again the boat miraculously remained right side up. Aside from learning to pump the sliding seat, the mechanics of pulling double was familiar to me from what could only be called contests between Nettie and myself at age twelve in the Rangely. But here there was the additional task of maintaining stability with the oars on the backstroke by skidding the bowls of the spoons along the surface. Thanks mainly to the smooth lagoon, I managed to plane my oars and keep us out of the drink.

Once we got into a rhythm with some way on, the experience became exhilarating instead of a losing game with Archimedes. Mona's stiletto split the surface so keenly that it left almost no wake until we had to turn, which presented a new challenge. And turning quickly became a necessity as we had nearly bisected the cove with just a dozen strokes. This called for level coordination and considerable room. Somehow we managed to alter course without getting wet. Soon we were zigzagging through the flotilla of canoes and dinghies, much to the consternation of their helmsmen who several times resorted to splashing us when their warning shouts failed to get our attention in time.

A half hour later, soaked with brine and perspiration, we collapsed on the beach, which was obligingly now just wide enough with the receding tide to spread our picnic blanket. While I sat trying to choke down my seeds by lubricating them with frequent spoonfuls of yogurt, I studied Mona's messy mop of straw, her rosy cheeks and painful stare, her twisted smile. Kooky as she was, I couldn't help admiring her for surviving, for making a life for herself and, yes, even for constructing the world's tippiest boat.

"I have an idea I'd like to bounce off you, Karcher," Mona began when we'd downed her roughage. "I propose that you and I blow the whistle on Auburn at Maine Medical. She's affiliated there. We might get a sympathetic ear and discover an avenue to discredit her."

"No good. They'll back her and accuse us of neurotic muckraking."

"Okay, how about we march in there with the whole crew?"

"Perhaps, but I'll wager a tenner the others chicken out or turn against us. I mean, how do you propose to pry Porcher from the pen and get her to kick her best friend in the ass? And are you willing to offer yourself up to old Harry so he'll pull out of Auburn long enough to listen? Sorry, that wasn't nice of me. But can you imagine convincing those two that Auburn is a fraud?"

"Sure. Set them at each other's throats for a bit. All it would take is letting Porcher know that Harry's sleeping with Auburn. Can't you just picture the fur flying?"

"I'm sure Porcher knows and doesn't care."

"All right, Mister Wet Blanket, what's your plan?"

"I haven't got one. Tell you the truth, I don't have the stomach for it, Mona. All I want is to get back with Witte and erase 1961 from memory."

"And what chance do you think you have of that if you let Auburn off the hook?"

"I'm hoping Witte'll trust me that it's over with Auburn."

"I hardly know your wife, Karcher, but she strikes me as one who needs more than a little convincing to change her mind."

"You're right there. She's got heavier flywheels than any woman I know."

Mona snickered. "That can work to your advantage. Hard to win; hard to lose. Slow to warm; slow to cool. I'll wager she can go all night if you wind her up easy."

"How do you know so much about what makes Witte tick?"

"All women need to be romanced, brought up to temperature slowly. Most men don't know that or are too impatient, so they never experience their woman's full potential."

"What's romance got to do with disposing of Auburn?"

"You just said you wanted to close that chapter of your life and get on with wooing Witte. I'm speaking to that."

"So I should send her a dozen roses?"

"Not a bad start."

"Witte's wily as a fox. She'd see right through that ploy. And, as you said yourself, she'll need something much more convincing than a bouquet."

"Of course. Lot's more. That's half the fun. Be creative and persistent."

"But what about this Auburn thing? All the offerings in the world won't erase my infidelity—correction: my attempted infidelity."

"Look, if you were still in love with Auburn you wouldn't be sending flowers, love letters and such to Witte, would you?"

"No."

"Well, don't you think she knows that you, like most mortals, can't be in love with more than one person at a time?"

"I guess so."

"Okay, so she'll interpret your ovations as a heart shift of allegiance and know that you've dumped Auburn. You don't have to lay Auburn's corpse on her doorstep."

"I'm not so sure. I still think Witte would be more convinced by a corpse than a bouquet."

"You sure don't know women very well, Karcher." Mona sighed and turned to face a fresh rattle of drums drifting from the Eastern Promenade. "Parade's tomorrow." She looked back with a distant stare. "I always wanted to march in a band like that with our horns blasting in harmony so loud that spectators lining the route would have to cover their ears. What power." Her focus pulled back to me. "Damn it, Karcher. I think honking a bugle would blow away my anger better than rowing, swimming or screaming. I'd like to stick its bell up Auburn's ass." She paused to reflect on Auburn's auditory defamation, shook her head and laughed in disgust. "Hell, she's not even worth wasting my breath on." The drums discharged a burst of distant thunder then resumed their desiccated crackle.

"Hey," she said, bouncing to her feet, "want to meet me at the parade tomorrow?"

I looked at Mona's baggy form and tried to envision her muscular body rippling under her soggy sweat suit, her square sneakered feet punching the pavement, a chrome-plated bugle pressed to her lips, blaring. Maybe in uniform,

I thought. She'd certainly have the stamina. "Sure," I said. "I love parades."

"Monument Square at ten, then."

I wanted to hug her for being such a good friend but feared I might upset her knife edge balance. A part of me was afraid that if we got physically close, the electricity might start, and neither of us needed any more confusion in our lives. Since we never discussed our feelings for one another, never tested our affection, we were able to maintain a level of mutual respect and admiration that lovers lose in loving.

We loaded up and wended our way back to the garage by way of the Prom. The Thunderheads were still drilling near the bandstand in the park. As we passed by perhaps three hundred yards above them, thirty horns flashed a phalanx of diamonds and seared the afternoon with their melancholy moan, fronted by a tireless rumble of tim-tom patterns, all choreographed by a solemn majorette blowing shrill signals on a chromium police whistle. We drove the rest of the way in silence. I helped her hang the shell from loops of rope she'd arranged over the car. When I had the oars paired and on my shoulders again, she stretched to touch my cheek. It was just a brush but it meant a lot to me.

"You're a good buddy, Karcher. Without you I'd probably be following Fred into the sea."

"Nonsense," I interjected. "You're too tough to quit."

I thought of Nettie and how keen life's edge hung in the balance. She had been tough too, but her lover had handed her a knife. Perhaps Mona's saving grace lay in keeping people at a safe distance, but I hoped instead it was her well-developed sense of self. I prayed that she had even half of Witte's core serenity to sustain her.

That night I lay awake pondering man's will to live and concluded that the decision to live or to take one's life rested within a tiny locked module centered in the solar plexus. The module was programmed at conception. Its circuits could not be altered. Outside influences could affect the timing of a suicide but not its certainty. Fred was a goner before he was born. Mona might survive. I too apparently would live out my term. Witte's fate was never in question.

* * * * * * * *

The Memorial Day parade down Congress Street heralded the true beginning of spring in Portland. For many it was the first time to open the apartment window, shed the coat and strut a lighter form in the sun. It was an excuse to smile and greet and loft balloons. It was opening day for children of all ages. And they were there, packing Monument Square, lining the sidewalks, leaning out of windows, perching on low roofs and on older people's shoulders.

I found Mona dressed in her pink sweat suit and sitting amongst the children on the curb. She was blowing bubbles from a huge wad of Bazooka gum. Her straw hair stood in spikes, exaggerating her surprised albino stare as though she had sat too long under a Van DeGraff generator.

"Hi, kids," I said, my eyes including the little ones on either side of her. "Great day for a parade, eh?"

A nine-year-old girl on Mona's immediate left made a disgusted expression and hissed. I looked directly into her dark eyes. "Lousy line, huh?"

The dour brunette nodded in Mona's direction. "You're just trying to pick up a girl."

"It happens that I know this young lady."

Mona was playing along with the gag, looking away and fidgeting. She burst a baseball-sized bubble and resumed chawing noisily with her mouth open.

"She don't know you, Mister. Get lost."

I squatted in front of my feisty opponent and studied the fierce lines of resistance in her face. "You know, I used to live with a woman a lot like you. I miss her terribly. This is my friend, Mona, and I'd like to sit between you both, if you don't mind."

The girl started to edge left, but then her mouth tightened. "Why aren't you with that woman you miss?"

Mona came to my rescue. "Karcher, here, and his wife are separated, Janet. We're just friends. I'd like him to sit with us."

Janet grimaced as she moved aside. I took my place on the curb between them, making myself as slim as possible. When I turned to thank Janet for her consideration, I noticed that she had folded her arms in resolute disapproval; so, I looked past her for a sign of the parade approaching. The lump returned to my throat as my focus slipped to her tiny hand clutching her arm and the lock of dark hair shading her face. Then I heard the drums: that deep, ominous rumble alternating with desiccated rattling.

A moment later the leading flags poked their golden staffs above the blacktop.

"Here they come," squealed Mona, jumping to her feet. Janet and I looked at each other for permission to stand and cheer. (I suddenly felt the need for her approval.) She nodded and began to rise but kept her eyes on me to be sure I followed suit. I did, and we quickly became caught up in the festivities.

The Thunderheads were front band, marching a respectful distance behind the color guard. They advanced inexorably with stately precision, blaring "With Flags Aloft" at a tempo fit for a coronation under strict orders from the same stern majorette who marked time by positioning her baton first to the prow of her helmet, then to her right shoulder, her left shoulder, and her naval before repeating the sequence. She was dressed all in white with gold braid trim. Her legs, bare from the tops of her boots to the hem of her skimpy satin skirt, were alternately breaking at the knee with martial restraint, floating her body as serenely as a swan glides on a still pond.

"Gawd, will you get a load of that statue!" I whooped.

"Karcher, ole buddy, I think that statue's your wife," Mona shouted above the relentless rhythm of the tim-toms.

"No, can't be," I countered, squinting to discern the features of the still too distant automaton whose eyes were barely visible beneath her paperboard helmet's visor. "Witte's never been involved with a band."

"She's beautiful," exclaimed Janet, "and look, she's starting to twirl."

The baton with which she had so eloquently postured suddenly became a fan of silver leaf, dancing about her. Without breaking the composure of her torso she made the baton fly from hand to hand, around her waist, over her head and between her legs, as if it were driven by an intricate, invisible linkage deriving power from the sun. Not once did she flinch or deflect her focus in spite of the tumultuous cheers and roaring applause from both sides of Congress Street.

When I caught sight of the Murch pout above the chin strap my heart kicked me so hard in my throat, I thought I was going to choke. I swallowed hard several times then launched myself from the curb and tried to scream, "Witte," but my voice broke up and drifted aloft like so many bubbles released from a child's loop. For a moment I stood alone several feet in front of the crowd, transfixed by Witte's uncompromising resolve.

Just before she pulled alongside, the blaring ceased and the drums switched to their forte/piano cadence. Witte stopped the baton as suddenly as she had begun twirling it and resumed marking time. Never during all those long seconds did I see her so much as flick her focus from the flag ahead, but at one point she seemed to catch her breath, and I saw her draw her bottom lip under her slightly spaced incisors.

"She's a gem, Karcher." It was Mona close behind me. Without thinking I turned and collapsed into her arms, sobbing. "Sh...she m...makes me go all w...weak inside."

Suddenly aware of my impropriety I pulled away and swabbed my eyes with the back of my hand. "Damn, that was dumb. Sorry, Mona."

"Sorry? What are friends for? Here." She handed me a tissue from her purse.

"Look, if you don't mind, I want to pace the band and catch her at the Promenade when they break up." Seeing the wild look in my eyes, Mona didn't try to detain me.

Janet, who had been taking all this in, piped up, "Can I come with you? Please? I want to meet her." I crouched and faced the girl who for but a few brush strokes could have been Witte at nine. Her serious dark eyes were searching mine, pleading without giving ground.

"Yes, I think you should," I said. "Come on." I took Janet's tiny hand and set out at a brisk walk to regain the Thunderheads.

"Don't forget the flowers," Mona called after us.

I was ambivalent about letting Witte see us following her and hung back alongside the bugles for awhile, peeking between their bells to catch glimpses of her ponytail swaying to her relentless grind. Her body was enough to inspire any band to march tirelessly for miles and her motion was so persuasive, it was no surprise that everyone kept in step, including Janet and me.

Oblivious of time and place and guided by my figurehead in white gold, I wove with Janet in tow through the surging spectators and the numerous vendors lining the parade route. I don't remember their faces except that none showed disapproval of our passage. Nor do I recall the marches the band played that we felt more than heard. The whole of my being was locked in sync with Witte.

Thus transported, I arrived at the Prom staging area, glowing but empty handed having marched several miles seemingly on thin air. Poor Janet was pooped; she plopped down on the grass and panted. The Thunderheads were breaking up near the bandstand where Mona and I had seen them drilling. Recalling Mona's advice, I flew into a panic.

"Oh, my God, Janet, I haven't any flowers. What'll I do?"

"How about them?"

Janet had jumped up with delight at being consulted and was pointing to the bandstand which was dripping with wisteria blossoms. As we came within range of their leguminous musk, my mind was transported back to the Varney green in June of 1959. I was standing under the wisteria trellis at our wedding ceremony, with the Reverend Donald Primm presiding. Verna was pounding the spinet as Witte on Loring's arm approached us with regal solemnity, leading her constituents in a double file procession.

"Are these okay?" Janet was stretching to break off a branch with three blossom clusters.

"Uh..., sure," I replied, coming out of my trance.

Janet laid the fall of flowers across my arm and smiled for the first time. " They smell kinda funny. I hope she likes 'em."

"They're perfect," I said, trying to hide my tears.

I heard a cheer rise from the disbanding Thunderheads and turned to see Witte, high on the broad shoulders of two of the drummers, waving her helmet and blowing kisses to the bandsmen swarming and wolf-whistling at her feet. The clasp was gone from her hair, and her face, flushed and beaming, radiated a girlish exhilaration I'd never seen. I was stagestruck by her presence and more than a little intimidated by the competition, but I forced myself to advance. Janet stayed right by my side.

After the men put Witte down, each member of the corps embraced her before parting. I waited until the last of them was gone before I made my move. Loring and Ida were waiting with Pattin, well to one side. Striding with all the confidence I could muster, I closed the fifty paces that remained between us.

"That was some performance," I began clumsily. "I mean, the whole thing. We saw it all." Janet nudged me. "Oh, excuse me. Witte, this is Janet, a devoted fan of yours. She asked to meet you." Janet nudged me again, harder. "And this is for you—from both of us." I approached to decorate my favorite soldier whose lower lip was now trembling. As I draped the wisteria bow across her right shoulder I heard for certain this time the rush of air when she caught her breath, and knew the spark was still alive. I stepped back quickly to preserve her dignity.

Witte locked her knees to stop their shaking, heaved a deep sigh and, looking directly at Janet, addressed us both with obvious difficulty. "Well—my goodness—thank you."

"I picked them myself," piped Janet proudly.

Witte looked back at me. Her eyes were brimming. "I see," she said with barely controlled gravity. "They're lovely, Missy."

Even Janet, squirming against my right leg, her face buried under my arm, sensed that Witte was coming apart. I desperately needed to experience her full disassembly and prayed that she'd disintegrate in my arms and allow me to carry her home. But Loring's last words in April— "Patience, Karcher. Patience, that's all."—challenged me to change the subject. I'm glad I did.

"I know you have an iron constitution, Witte, but how in hell can you tolerate such prolonged auditory overload without ear protection?"

Witte reached in her jacket pocket and withdrew a pair of waxed cotton ear plugs. "Daddy wears these when huntin'. Try 'em, dear." When she presented her fist, barely larger than Janet's, and dropped the warm, sticky stoppers in my hand, I had to fight the urge to seize her slender wrist, draw her to me and crush her in my arms. It was a shaky pair of hands that worked the plugs into my ears then quickly withdrew into hiding behind my back.

Witte clapped her hands close to my right ear. "See?"

"Hey," I exclaimed with misdirected enthusiasm, "these are almost as good as my chain saw muffs."

"Stop shouting," admonished Janet.

I laughed heartily for the first time since our separation. Witte had met her match and seemed to enjoy Janet's pluck as much as my foolishness. Both she and Janet began giggling and making silly faces at me.

I had just reached to pull the plugs and restore order when I felt Loring's heavy hand on my shoulder. "What do you think of our drum major, son?" I turned to see Ida glaring at me from under Loring's wing. Pattin was smiling and batting the beads on her new stroller as if to cancel her grandmother's disapproval. I stooped to pick her up, but the stroller suddenly reversed, pulling my daughter out of reach. Her tiny deep vee smile faded to a perplexed pout, but the proximate beads distracted her before the disappointment fully registered.

"She times them steady as the Klein, sir," I replied, pushing Ida's punishment aside. "Mighty impressive. I always knew she had a strong beat." I looked at Witte. She smirked for a second but quickly hid her mirth, hearing her mother's biting remark closely follow my compliment.

Referring to Witte's heartbeat, Ida snapped, "Too strong, when it comes to men."

A terrible silence fell over the remaining six standing by the bandstand in the strong afternoon sun. Loring kicked at the ground and shook his head. Witte looked daggers at her mother. Pattin was nodding off. And I tried to disappear.

Janet stopped fidgeting to give Witte a peck on the cheek and whisper something in her ear. Witte smiled, patted her on the rump and sent her on her way. Janet gave me a shrug and ran off in the direction of the observatory. My eyes followed her small, flailing figure until it disappeared over the hill.

A sinking feeling settled in the pit of my stomach. I was no longer faced with having to win back one Murch woman, but two. And it wasn't going to be easy.

Chapter 16

RESTART

Pattin's ebullience was no match for the morose Murch facades. But then, how could she be expected to fathom the gravity of her father's indiscretion? I chose to view her cheer as a mark of well-deserved trust and stuck my neck out a little further.

"I'm so glad I ran into you folks," I said, forcing myself to smile and look briefly at each one, saving Loring for last. My eyes stayed with him as I continued. "I have something to share with you all, but I need to speak to Witte alone first."

"She's heard enough of your tales." Ida grabbed Witte's arm and started for the truck.

"Just a minute, there," Loring warned. "The boy's trying to explain himself. Give him a chance."

Witte snapped her arm out of her mother's grip and turned on her. "I'll *hear* what he has to say, *now*, in the bandstand."

"*Well*, I never." Ida stormed for the truck, took her place in the passenger's seat, slammed the door and sat, grimly waiting.

Loring shook his head. "She'll simmer down by supper. Why don't you come for a bite, Karcher — if you can tolerate our company."

Witte looked anxious and tugged at my sleeve. "Can you mind Pattin, Daddy? I'll be along in a minute." She started for the bandstand at flank speed. I followed behind to enjoy again her devastating sway. When she reached the top step she nodded in the direction of the wisteria and moved to take a seat under it.

"I'll stand if you don't mind," I said, trying to ignore the wisteria's intoxicating perfume. Witte crossed her legs, looked up with an inquisitive slant to her eyebrows and waited.

"It's over, Witte,...."

Before I could add, "between Auburn and me," she went white. Her mouth fell open and her eyes began to search my face in desperate disbelief.

"Honest. I haven't seen her since mid March when we had our termination appointment."

Witte recovered instantly. "And did you terminate her, dear?"

"No, but Mona and I had planned to discredit her until we realized how difficult that would be. We thought..."

"We?"

"Mona and I. We reasoned that the important thing was to wrest ourselves from Auburn's web, put it all behind us and go on with our lives."

"I see." Witte was breathing with agitation. "And that was Mona I saw you with at the Square?"

"Yes. So? She's been a good buddy during this trying period." Seeing Witte's eyes narrow, I added, "No, we're not lovers. Not even close. Mona's a lesbian, for God's sake."

"I see."

"For Chrissakes, Witte, give me a break. *You're* the only one that can turn my insides to Jello."

"Zat so?"

"Look, it was you that insisted I get mixed up with that bitch doctor."

"I don't plan on making that kind of mistake again."

"Does that mean you'll come home with me?"

"Not so fast, Buster."

A prolonged blast of the Ford's Klaxon put a temporary hold on our discussion.

"I've got to go, dear. Come by about four, if you like. We're havin' chicken." She rose and clattered down the steps, out across the field to the truck, leaped over the tailgate and took her seat in the bed with her back to the cab. Her eyes followed me as the AA Ford putted past the bandstand but she made no other parting gestures. In the cab, Ida was staring straight ahead, and Pattin, bobbing in her lap, was doing her best to untie her grandmother's bonnet strap.

* * * * * * * *

Loring answered my knock at the door. "Well, don't just stand there gawkin'. Come in, boy. Come in." His warm, brusque manner momentarily steadied the queasy stomach I'd worked up since the aftermath of the parade, allowing a few words of greeting to pass my lips before I streaked for the bathroom and lost the remains of my lunch.

I must have looked dreadful when I returned to the kitchen because Ida left her post at the stove and lunged for the nearest chair to place it under my sagging butt. Witte rushed to my side to steady my descent. And Loring was right there with a glass of ice cold Coke. "Sip that slow, son."

I lifted the glass and pretended to sample the bubbly brown liquid. My hand was shaking so, I spilled most of it down my chin and across my clean white turtleneck. Witte couldn't decide whether to use the moistened paper towel she had in her hand to wipe my brow or to mop up my pullover. After several false moves she chose the garment. The gentle pressure of her hand patting my chest, the smell of her hair and the sound of her breathing quieted my nerves better than any tranquilizer.

"Feelin' better, dear?"

"Yes, much. Thanks." I risked a glance at Ida who had settled into the chair next to me.

"Took a bad turn, did you, Karcher?" Ida's eyebrows were almost vertical with concern.

"I guess it was just fear of being abandoned again. Darned old tapes are hard to erase. Sorry."

"Oh, I guess we'll forgive you—*this* time," Witte said with a wink.

Like an army nurse, Ida tended enemy sick as she did her own. "Go lie down in the guest room for awhile, Karcher. Don't mind the mess." She helped me up and stayed with me while I wobbled the few paces to the back bedroom where I'd slept when first I visited the farm.

Pattin's crib was wedged in the far corner, and Witte's clothes were bulging from the Wedgewood blue armoire. The bed was unmade and redolent of Yardley's English Lavender. I sank to the rumpled sheets and curled into a fetal tuck, hugging Witte's pillow. I felt gentle hands untying my shoes and slipping them off then drawing up the comforter and tucking it around my shoulder. The door latch clicked, switching off the tape loop inside my head, and I fell asleep.

When I awoke an hour and a half later, my shaking had ceased and with it the chill of anxiety. The aroma of chicken potpie was irresistible. I laid quietly a while longer, reliving the childhood thrill of waking in the late afternoon after a bout with the flu to find myself hungry for the first time in a week and savoring the smell of Nettie's slumgullion drifting up the back stairs to my room over the garage.

The door creaked open ever so slowly until it was sufficiently ajar to admit Witte's long face listing hard to port. "You awake?" she whispered. "Supper's 'bout ready."

Pattin's round face appeared much lower in the opening, and before Witte could stop her, our daughter had slipped through and toddled up to the bed, pointing and chanting, "Da-da, Da-da." This time when I reached for her, no one pulled her away. Once in my arms she fell still except for one tiny hand that kept working the cowlick over my right temple.

"She misses you," Witte said from the doorway.

"Come, join us for a moment." I stretched my free arm towards her. Witte advanced cautiously, keeping her eyes on me, and crawled in alongside Pattin. When I felt her thighs press against mine, I knew I was being forgiven.

The Waltham Regulator in the kitchen bonged six times and resumed its comforting tick. Witte stroked my cheek with a fragrant finger. "Can you eat, dear?"

"You bet," I said, scooping up Pattin and raising her at arm's length over my head, which elicited a big grin followed by giggling that resulted in her drooling on my nose. "After I devour this little doll." I blew in her exposed navel. Pattin erupted with such a fit of giggles she began to hiccup.

"Go easy, Karcher. She just ate."

"Yes, ma'am."

I quickly tipped Pattin upright and set her on the floor beside the bed then took her hand and led her into the kitchen. Feeling her brace to balance her wide-track stagger, made all the more unsteady by her upturned, smiling face, erased the last vestige of my self-pity. For here was someone who not only unconditionally accepted me but depended on my being there for her. And so it was with considerable confidence that I also braced to face my uncertain future.

Witte took Pattin from me at the pantry door and headed upstairs to wash and change her, leaving me alone with her mother. Ida was between the pantry and the table with a fistful of flatware. Before I could acknowledge her presence she had assessed my condition and begun setting our places. Without looking up, she reported, "Your color come up good, Karcher. When I tucked you in, you was peaked as a perch."

"Yes—well—I feel more like a lion after my nap. Boy, that pie smells good."

"Loring said you was a big help with the 'quipment last month." Ida was still not looking at me.

"I'm afraid he wasn't so pleased at the time."

Ida stopped setting the table and turned to look out the window. "Yes, I heard about that, too.

"You could have killed him, Karcher."

I couldn't see her face, but I could tell she was on the verge of tears by the cadence of her voice.

"My brother Perley, he wa'n't so lucky as Loring. He was alone, plowin' uphill. Blade struck a boulder. Before he could get the clutch down, that tractor reared up and over it went. Pinned him in the furrow. Crushed his chest.

"Neighbor found him. He was dead three, two hours. Doctor couldn't do nothin'."

Ida turned back and resumed setting the table. Though I tried not to stare at her, I couldn't help noticing the puddles of pain in her large, dark eyes, the twist of her eyebrows, and especially how the corners of her small mouth drooped to block the anguish she was determined not to show.

"Loring went and got Perley's tractor. I told him to leave it sit for the scrap scroungers, but Loring — you know — he can't stand to see machinery in distress. Said he needed it for hayin'. She's still stuck out there — the Farmall — back of the barn."

"Ida, I'm so sorry. I didn't know."

Still without looking up, Ida continued, "Life's precious, Karcher. Love, too. If it weren't for Loring, I'd be in pieces and under ground.

"He cares lot about you, Karcher. Hurt him awful when you and Witte broke up." She put the chicken pie in the center of the table. I saw her take a peek at me before quartering it with quick strokes of the knife.

"Witte, she's been a wreck. Poor thing's hardly eaten in three months. Buried herself in that band." She set out the salad. "Course, she wouldn't let on. Kept it all inside."

Hearing Witte returning, Ida moved closer to me and whispered, "Many a night I hear her cryin' in there when I come down to stoke the stove." She nodded toward the guest room then brandished the spoon in her hand. "You better fix it—and quick."

I had planned to briefly relate the news of my breaking off with Auburn over supper, but it seemed Ida wasn't aware of the depth of my involvement which left me with a dilemma. Should I start from scratch and drag them through the entire episode or avoid the subject entirely and announce my plan for our reunion: making over the boathouse into our new home? Neither plan looked promising. Recounting risked further alienation, and presumption of a reconciliation might backfire. Witte had had only a few hours to reset her mind, and a premature proposal could cement her resistance.

"I think I already have," I answered Ida, ambiguously.

Witte entered the room carrying Pattin, freshly scrubbed and wearing a seersucker nightgown. "Say good night to Daddy."

I kissed my daughter on the cheek and received another big grin.

"She's awful cranky," Witte said, heading for the back bedroom. "Too much excitement."

"G'night, sunshine," I called, waving to the beaming kewpie peeking over her mother's shoulder.

"Livin' doll, that one," boomed Loring from the laundry doorway. He stumped to the pump and took a couple swipes at the handle, splashed water in his face and mopped it away with his bandanna. "Smells good, Ida."

Witte reappeared in skin-tight Levis chained at the waist and fairly bursting her bodice of white cotton cord. Her hair was drawn back and loosely secured with a bone clasp, exposing her ears and neck. She trailed a subversive wake of Russia Leather. And she'd only been out of my sight two minutes.

"I'm hungry," she said to her mother and winked wickedly in my direction before sitting down.

Although I'd witnessed Witte's sudden transformations dozens of times, my astonishment was as fresh as the first. I was standing behind my chair at the foot of the table when her perfume hit me. Feeling my knees start to buckle, I gripped the ladder back and hung on.

Loring was already seated facing me. At Witte's entrance his eyebrows rose in unison and remained elevated for several seconds. "Whooof," he said before digging in. It needed no translation.

Ida never missed a chance to get in a dig. "Well, look who's on the prowl."

"I'm not, either," Witte snapped, her cutaway nostrils flaring, eyes flashing black as ice on a still mill pond. "We have a guest for supper."

Ida knew when to quit. Her eyes dropped to her plate, and she stuffed her mouth full of pie as if to stifle the retort forming there before it escaped her lips.

Loring was sifting through his second mouthful of chicken when he detected a foreign object. After much mastication and chortling, which drew all eyes in mutual concern, he managed to segregate the culprit and swallow the remains. Much to everyone's relief he then produced a bone chip Ida had missed in the mix. "Must I eat the beak, Ida?" he growled. An uneasy chuckle of relief erupted on all quarters.

"Hey," I ventured, taking advantage of the distraction after receiving such a clear message from Witte, "I have a proposal to make."

Before I could lay the building blocks on the table, Witte came back, "You already did that, dear."

"Can't hurt to do it again," I said, pushing back my chair and dropping to my knees at her side with a napkin ring in my hand. Witte drew her arm back and peered down at me, wearing the quizzical expression of a long-eared owl. My eyes were about level with her armpit, affording me a clear view through the stretched opening in her sleeveless top.

"Witte Murch, I request...I beg you..." My eyes filled and my voice faltered.

I cleared my throat and began again. "I know I haven't been worthy of your trust and affection lately, but that was an aberration. I want us to restart the fire. Will you, Witte Murch, remain my wife? I need you in my life. No one else will do."

Witte took my face in her hands and gently held it still while her eyes searched mine. "I liked what you said, dear. But what's that 'aberration'?"

"A temporary excursion of the soul, Witte."

Her eyes ceased their scanning and narrowed. "And what's to prevent another – aberration?"

"Boundaries," I said, confidently. "You taught me that, remember?

"A person develops boundaries to insulate the soul. It's a matter of identity. Take yourself for example. You know exactly who you are. Your soul is inviolate. You have boundaries." My gaze dropped again to her arm pit. "Boy, do you have boundaries."

The view under Witte's bodice proved so distracting that I had to move back to my chair to concentrate.

"Where was I? Oh, yes. Now. One develops boundaries—a sense of self—very early in life. In a stable and loving home such as yours a child develops strong boundaries. In a chaotic home environment such as mine, the child is never sure what to be, how to act. He develops weak boundaries or none at all. That leaves his soul vulnerable to insidious influences."

Witte's eyes were becoming ever wider but their focus never left me. She slid back in her chair and appeared to brace herself for the rest of my delivery.

"While repeated attacks on a soul with fragile boundaries often drive its occupant insane, sometimes the reverse happens: the patient finds himself. It can be a most joyous occasion to learn who you are after years of attempting to emulate others who don't have your best interests at heart. I speak from experience."

Loring's visible agitation had reached the breaking point. "Damn it, Stickney, (smack, smack) have you given up that woman or not?"

"I most certainly have, sir. I terminated our sessions last March and have had no contact whatever with her since. She was a sorceress. If I had the money, I'd sue her for malpractice."

Ida heaved a great sigh. "Well, that's it, then. It's settled. I don't want to hear another word about it. Eat up good before everything gets cold."

I looked over at Witte. She was squirming. Her face was flushed and pouring sweat, and her knuckles were white from vise-gripping the seat of her chair. In her dilated pupils I saw the flames. "I...I do. I mean, I will," she said in an earthy whisper.

"Do? Will? Will what, Witte?" bellowed Loring without looking up from his food.

Ida's eyes slowly lifted from her plate. "You haven't touched your chicken, dear." Her gaze rose to meet her daughter's raging pupils. "Good Lord, Loring, I think she's thrown a fever?"

Fortunately neither Loring nor Ida recognized Witte's symptoms, which I could see she was desperately trying to suppress. She had apparently been working up one of her solo orgasms during my oratory and was about to pop. Before her parents reached her side, Witte croaked, "I'll be fine," pushed her chair back and bolted for the guest room.

"I'll see what's the matter," I said, trying to sound clinically concerned as I left the table.

I found Witte prostrate on the bed, tangled in the sheets, writhing. She was biting her lower lip and panting, which produced a sputtering hiss like a factory whistle trying to speak on a manifold full of condensate. Her scent, driven to aphrodisiac potency by runaway hormones, had already filled the room. She clutched at the edges of the mattress as if she were trying to pull herself deeper into the kapok. "Don't," she groaned, hearing the door close and my footsteps approaching.

It had been almost two years since I'd witnessed Witte's throttle stick wide open and the first time I'd seen her lose control in public. If there was a crumb of coal left lurking in my heart, this display of spontaneous combustion vaporized it. I was on fire from my scalp to my toenails.

"I still can't believe the effect we have on one another," I said, standing a safe distance from the foot of the bed. "When we're in the same room I feel like I'm being peppered with white hot magnesium dust sprayed from a giant sparkler. When we're apart I ceaselessly search for you in every woman my eyes can resolve."

Witte began to shudder and murmur. "Oh...oh, no...no." She buried her face in the pillow, plunged her hands between the mattress and box spring, arched her elbows and pulled with all her might. When I heard her muffled moan and saw her body go limp I knew it was safe for me to approach. Kneeling over her, I kissed her damp nape then swept aside the hair that stuck to her temple and cheek. She rolled onto her back, pulled a ragged breath and stretched a trembling tapered finger to touch my lips. "I've missed you awful, awful bad, Karcher."

Chapter 17

MOONSTONE

"We ought to finish supper," I said, trying to ignore the surge of testosterone flooding my senses. I rose from the bed and adjusted my baggy chinos to minimize the prominence.

Witte tried to sit up. She got her elbows braced under her then gave up and flopped back down. "I'm too weak, dear. Could you fetch me a glass of orange juice from the fridge?"

"Sure. Be back in a sec."

I opened the door, stuffed my hands deep in my pockets and strolled into the kitchen. Ida was fussing with the stove and seemed relieved to see me. "She's okay," I said casually. "Just ran low on fuel. Needs some orange juice to get her started."

"I shouldn't wonder, poor thing. Her supper's warmin' in the oven along with the rest of yours." Ida poured a glass of juice and held it out to me. "Here, dear. This'll pick her right up."

For a second I stood contemplating the frosty jigger in Ida's hand, wondering how I was going to take it from her without revealing my condition. "Uh...tell you what," I said, shifting my weight from one foot to the other. "Why don't *you* take it to her. I think she'd enjoy some soothing words from her mother."

"That's kind of you, Karcher. I will."

I spent the next few minutes pacing the kitchen, trying to talk myself down. The thing that finally worked was an image of Auburn commiserating with Porcher about my inability to get it up.

And not a moment too soon. Loring appeared at the door just as the women were emerging from the guest room, Witte on her mother's arm.

"Feelin' better, Missy?"

"Yes, Daddy. I just gotta eat somethin'."

"Sit right down, you two," Ida ordered, passing my pale and shaky wife from her grasp to mine. She extracted our parched pies from the oven and followed us as we shuffled to the table like a pair of octogenarians. "I think the both of you've been apart long enough," she observed. I tingled all over as the last barrier came down.

It was the longest meal in history but well worth the agony. When it was over and cleaned up, Witte and I excused ourselves to take a drive and catch up on the details of our lives apart.

* * * * * * * *

The full moon was just rising when I wiped the dew from the windshield. We slipped into the Ford and sat apart awhile in silence, watching the huge orange ball turn pale and bright and small as it broke from the pines and climbed to put out the stars. The night was so still that the aspen leaves cast sharp shadows on the kitchen shutters. We could hear Doak's dalmatian howling a quarter mile to the south. A lone bull frog called three times from the pond and fell silent.

Witte slid closer, grasped the top of the steering wheel with her right hand and pulled herself around to face me. Her hand relaxed its grip but remained on the rim. "Let's drive to the beach, dear. It's a beautiful night."

I was so taken by the exquisiteness of the small hand before me in the moonlight that I didn't respond at first, and when I did, it was to address form instead of function. "Why couldn't man craft an engine with curves like this?" I said, taking her hand from the wheel and working it between my fingers, noting its diminutive yet perfect proportions and the long oval nails devoid of polish that mirrored the lines of her face.

Witte pulled her hand away and scowled. "And what kind of 'lectricity do you suppose you'd get from me, Buster, if I was cast in bronze?"

"Bronze is a poor spark generator, Witte. I prefer iron."

"Karcher, if ever you should come to your senses—and I'm not sure I can wait that long—you'll discover that women make better lovers than engines."

Witte withdrew as far as she could without getting out of the car. She folded her arms, drew up her lower lip and, staring straight ahead, ordered: "Now, get started if you plan on spending another minute of your life with *this* woman."

I shoved up the spark and trod on the Ford's starter before she changed her mind.

"You know," I said, when the Model A was up to speed
a half mile down Broad Turn, "I was just kidding back
there."

"You weren't either."

At the Burnham Road intersection I could feel Witte's
eyes turn on me from the dark recess of the cab.

"Look, I know you're scared of the human body,
Karcher. You couldn't go through what you did as a child
without bein' affected." She paused and looked away.
When she resumed speaking, her voice was gentle and
seemed to come from the floorboards. "I guess I thought I
could show you different."

I reached for her hand and she let me take it. There was
no way I could verbalize an answer so I pressed her
trembling fingers to my lips one at a time. As I kissed each
one in turn I heard her sip suddenly five times in response,
after which she released a prolonged sob-sigh. My pleasure
at her reaction was peaked as much by the moonlit motion
of her creamy camisole as it was by the inch she edged
toward me.

Continuing to hold her hand to my lips, I drew each
fingertip into my mouth to taste and trace its tiny bud. And
she responded with a crescendo of sighs, moving ever
closer until she was almost in my lap. With her free hand
she began stoking my nape. I stole another peek and
noticed that the curl had returned to her upper lip, just to
the right of center.

My head went light and for a moment felt like it was
taking leave of my neck. When the horizon leveled, the
Ford was straddling the center line and weaving like a

drunken sailor. I wrenched the wheel to recover my lane and accidentally bit Witte's pinky in the process. Her yowl at close range made the car dart again across the yellow line. I yanked the wheel just in time to avoid a collision with an oncoming car and steadied out in my lane at thirty-five.

The ringing in my right ear had just about subsided when Witte put me straight. "Cemetery's just a mile ahead on the right. If you're careful, you can make it."

"Jeezus, Witte. Couldn't you have put that another way?"

Ordinarily I would have enjoyed her quip, but life at that moment seemed unusually precious, and the vision of crumbling shale slabs stippling a moonlit knoll made me shudder. I felt suddenly alone and too far from civilization. Backlighted by the moon, the pines lining the left side of the road stood starkly, black and thick against the hoary field beyond. The road climbed and bent left until the moon was dead ahead. Its icy disk drained the color from our faces. I watched as Witte's lips, now a ghastly gray, parted to answer.

"I don't know about you, Karcher. I just don't know."

"What?" I blurted in terror, hearing Witte's reedy voice distorted by a querulous quaver that issued from the wrinkled face of my maternal grandmother who appeared to have taken her place. "What don't you know about me?"

"Whether I can live with you," said the wizened widow in a steadier and considered tone from her revised perch more than a foot to my right.

My stomach sloshed against my diaphragm. I gulped a few breaths. As the oxygen reached my brain, my grandmother's furrowed mask melted and ran to reform the almond oval of Witte's face. Much relieved, I ventured a reply.

"I can't promise you an easy life with me, and I don't know how long I have to live, but this I can assure you: no one has *ever* elevated me to such pinnacles of joy and driven me to such depths of despair as you. That has to count for something."

"When I want to ride a roller coaster, Karcher, I go to the Beach." Witte paused, and I caught a glimpse of her incisors. "Which reminds me," she went on. "We haven't ridden the Dragon since 1954, our first summer together."

"Oh, no."

"Scared? I should think you'd be used to ups and downs." Witte was now kneeling on the seat, facing me and bouncing at the resonant frequency of the Ford's suspension, which caused the flivver to rock and steer a sinusoidal path despite my checks at the wheel.

"Stop it, Witte. You'll have us in the ditch."

"Promise you'll go coastin' with me," she taunted, continuing to pump her torso.

"Okay. Okay. Once. That's all. Now sit still."

Witte bent forward, nipped my ear and whispered, "I like your seesaw, sir," then settled back in the seat, cuddled up and continued in mock reflection: "Let's see. Once I figure your mood rhythm, I'll appear when you're up and scat before you take a header. But at the rate you cycle I'll have to stay awful close to be punctual. So I guess I might as well live with you. Huh?" She looked up with a kittenish smirk, her head tipped to one side while she waited for confirmation.

We were approaching the Route 1 intersection. I was too choked up to speak so I squeezed her hand and blinked to drain my eyes before the floodlights from the Mobil station revealed my tears. We puttered down through Blue Point and out across the Scarborough marsh flats. It wasn't until we had breasted the Snow cannery that I could find the words to answer her. Thickly but without hesitation I said, "I take it you're willing to compromise your principles and give our relationship another try."

"Maybe."

Before I could chastise myself for pressing her for commitment, a little hand was placed on my right knee and immediately began creeping up my thigh. In trying to slow its advance I pressed myself back into the seat, flooring the throttle in the process. But since the Ford was then lugging along East Grand at twenty miles per hour in high, its response was, thankfully, more audible than locomotive. With the onset of rod rattle the hand was quickly withdrawn. Witte separated herself and struck an innocent pose facing dead ahead, hands clasped tight in her lap. I lifted my foot, and the Model A chuffled the last half mile in grateful silence. Finding no parking spot along East Grand, I wasted a dollar to park in the Seven Seas lot across from Dave's, the deli where Witte had worked the summer we met.

Although it was early in the season with the Canadian crush still a month off, Old Orchard was seething with scantily clad girls trailing cheap but tantalizing perfume to lure their men who ogled and whistled from the latticed shadows along the White Way. Ahead, the throb and intermittent clatter of the Dragon punctuated by discordant screams, sucked us south toward the pier.

Witte tried towing me across the intersection to the coaster but broke her grip on my hand when I resisted and turned left toward the carousel. Wheeling around, she stamped her foot and hissed, "Oh, no, you don't, Buster."

"Give me a half hour to settle my supper, Witte. Okay? Then we'll go on it. I promise."

Witte squinted and moved in on me without breaking eye contact. I was so hypnotized by her commanding stare that I froze in her gaze until her narrow-set eyes became one and I was able to discriminate her scent from the cotton candy, the creosote and the sea.

"I'm no dumb Dora, Karcher," she croaked so close that I could hear her glottis clicks. Her hair, disturbed by the gentle onshore breeze, brushed my cheek and neck. "Once that organ gets a grip on you, I'd have to burn the pier down to get your attention."

Witte's approach and delivery were so intimate, I couldn't help feeling she intended more than privacy with her proximity. Normally in such circumstances, enraged and oblivious of her surroundings, she'd stand and deliver from where my remark stopped her, arms akimbo, voice raised sufficiently to close the gap. I sensed the stakes were higher this time, higher even than when we were courting.

She was standing perhaps an inch in front of me, and her breath was unbearably tickling my throat, but I dared not move. Her eyes, no longer accusing, had become mirrors of molten metal. Each reflected the face of a man framed in swirling lights. It was a stereo portrait of love mistrusted.

At first I didn't recognize the man's face as mine, it showed such age and pain: the brow furrowed with fear; the eyes red with anguish; the lips pale and pencil thin.

Was this what had become of me: this premature prune, wrinkled before its time, rejected for its bitter sweetness? Was I that locked between trust and love, forever frozen from the flesh like an iron ingot celibately cast? I shuddered and closed my eyes to block the image.

During my brief blackout, the strong scent of lavender and wood smoke restored my youth, and I reawakened to find Witte's crown almost touching my nose. I bent to kiss her forehead, but she jumped back, grabbed my hand and began towing me toward the beach.

"Hey, where are we going?" I called ahead.

"To consummate the marriage, dear."

"I thought you wanted to ride the Dragon."

"That can wait. This can't."

We hit the soft sand at full flail. Witte pulled erratically now as her feet lost and regained traction. Before reaching the high tide mark, she veered left toward the pier, slowing to a lope as she entered its shadow. I stumbled after her into the wind-eroded undulations between the pilings. Not far to my right the moonlit sea tossed plumes of silver spray to the rafters as it broke over the footings. Overhead and just to the left the blackened timbers amplified the dependable trombone of the carousel, inside whose engine room Witte and I had first explored the limits of our passion.

When we were deep under the pier Witte wheeled again to face me. Her lips were sealed but her chest heaved mightily with each breath that rushed through her flared nostrils. In the breeze her eyes, the size of the moon and charged with its light, glowed defiantly under a shifting veil of silk. Never once did she leave my gaze or stop to brush her hair aside as she worked to free the buttons on my shirt.

"Here?" I said, incredulous.

"Yuh," she inhaled, parting her lips just long enough to draw the word in, her fingers all the while pursuing my undoing.

I could see by the inclination of her eyebrows and the set of her bottom lip that I was under attack, but I was too absorbed with her paradoxically fierce femininity to respond until she reached the last button and began to unlace my belt.

"Whoa, Witte. We're in public. Are you nuts?"

As my eyes adjusted to the light, groping pairs began to pop from the shadows. They seemed to have us surrounded. It's a wonder we didn't trip on anyone in our headlong plunge into the grotto. The couple closest to our entry path had engaged the nearest piling in their lovemaking, using it as a brace for their athletic gyrations. I turned away quickly, hoping they hadn't seen me watching them.

"Gawd, Witte. This is barbaric. They're...they're doing it everywhere—on the beach, some half in the breakers, and that couple is using a piling for support." I nodded over my shoulder. "The sand. The barnacles. It's all so abrasive."

"Simmer down, dear."

"I feel like we've stumbled into a school of grunion that have just wriggled ashore to spawn during the full moon. Can't we go somewhere private?"

"Like inside the carousel?" Witte's nose wrinkled and tiny creases appeared alongside her eyes and vertically beside her mouth.

"Who's bunking in number Two Kinney?"

"The girls that replaced me and Kitty at Dave's, I guess."

"Do you suppose they'd...?"

"Look, if you want a bed that bad, we can go back to the apartment."

"N...no. I just don't feel comfortable around all these people."

I didn't dare tell her how scared I was, more even than on our first date. It wasn't the setting that was intimidating, really; that was just inappropriate, almost disgusting. It was Witte I was afraid of. If I so much as fluffed a move this time, I was sure I'd lose her for good, and more than anything in the world at that moment I wanted her to stay. I couldn't bear the thought of living alone without her.

"I don't think they're watching us, dear."

"That's not the point. It's that I need...time." I couldn't say courage.

"Time? We have the rest of the night. The sea isn't going anywhere."

"Thank you for being so patient with me, Witte."

She was anything but: eyes smoking; chest pounding; hands under my shirt, gliding all over my torso. I prayed she'd auto-climax and reduce pressure to a tractable level, allowing me time to pull myself together. But she'd built up such a head of steam waiting for me that it seemed cruel to request a postponement. And so with trembling, icy fingers I reached for the impossibly slender, ribbed waist band of her sweater.

No sooner had I grasped the warm hem when, as if on cue, the carousel's Wurlitzer began pounding the opening bars of "Mi Teresita," a heart-rending waltz written at the turn of the century by Teresa Carreno for her small daughter. I knew what was coming and froze, unable to raise my arms.

Once the bass drum finished setting the tempo, the achromatic glockenspiel attempted a glissando then trilled triumphantly. It was tiny Teresa performing her first recital.

My heart leaped to my throat. I swallowed hard and tried again to doff Witte's sweater, but the holztrompette stole the child's voice and began to bawl the verse in tight two-part harmony, breaking the last barrier to my heart. I burst into tears and collapsed in Witte's arms.

As I clung to her, the relentless Wurlitzer repeated the chorus three times without pausing for breath and then, as if to insure that my heart was truly broken, tacked on a prolonged coda of minor chords with all stops drawn. As the chords chromatically descended, each differed from the one before by just one semitone until the last, which resolved abruptly in a major key, leaving behind a lopsided patter of worn pump rods–"ticka-tacka, ticka-tacka, ticka-tacka..."—to restart my heart.

"I love you so much, I'm afraid to touch you," I sobbed. Isn't that crazy?"

Witte gave me a hug and another dose of reality therapy. "We're both crazy, dear. You for tryin' to replace your mother with a lover. Me for trying to play both roles. Long as we keep this up we're going to be hittin' and missin' like a one-lunger."

"Don't do me any favors," I snapped, pulling away and snuffing back my tears. "Nettie is the *last* person in the world I'd want you to emulate."

"Not Nettie as she was but the mother you wish she'd been."

"And if you were this ideal mother, do you think I'd want to make love to you?"

"'Course not; that's your...our problem."

"You mean, when you're my mommy, I can't get it up?"

"Yuh."

"Great. So I'm doomed to impotence because I didn't have a real mommy. Guess you'd better look for a new husband then, the product of a stable marriage." I paused hoping Witte would break in, but when she didn't I dug the trench deeper between us.

"I can picture you interviewing the new prospects now, forehead furrowed, eyes piercing their tender armor, the words hissing from between your lower teeth: 'Were you raised by a strict nanny who slept in your mother's room? Did your mother touch you only when delivering discipline? Did she often fail to produce your meals because she was drunk or subdued with Thorazine? Did she repeatedly threaten to kill herself? And did she then take her life in the house in front of the family with a butcher knife?'

"'Was it your father alone who cradled and stroked you, sang to you, cried with you and called you darling? Was he too an alcoholic? And did he die prematurely of a broken heart when you were seventeen?'"

Witte stiffened and scowled. "That's enough, Karcher." Her eyes narrowed to slits. "You think you're a major mystery, don't cha?" Her lower teeth began to show. "Well, let me tell you something, Buster." Her chest was heaving again but not from ardor. "I can see right through you. You're a jackal whimpering over your prey. Inside that bag-of-bones body, behind that hang-dog mask, you've got a vise grip on life. So don't think you can whine sympathy out of me."

"I'll be goddamned. You *are* Nettie risen from the dead in the body of an angel. The same accusations. The same metaphors. Even the same inflection in your voice. No wonder I picked you for my wife."

"Wife, yes. Mother, no. It's over, Karcher. I'm not going to bust myself up anymore. Not for you, not for anyone." She tipped her head toward me so that her eyes were barely visible under their heavy lids. "And I'm no angel, either."

Again right on cue the organ began to slash me "With Sword and Lance." As the brusk bars of the Sousa march cut into my spleen, I cursed myself for attacking Witte just when she was struggling with her allegiance to me.

Or so I thought. For it was I and not Witte who lacked insight into his partner's soul. My weak ego simply refused to recognize that Witte's loyalty had never been in question. Her apparent lapses in devotion were merely pauses to express frustration with my behavior. And more than a few of her outbursts I now suspect were staged in an attempt to educate me. If she had wanted to give me up for good she'd have done it long ago. Witte seldom put up with adversity.

But I was so taken with my plight at the time, I couldn't see past her grim facade.

"You don't know me at all," I protested. "That organ reminds me of what I want to be: a machine. A churning, gear gnashing, pounding engine—as nonhuman as possible. When I hear it I feel whole, inviolable, invincible.

"And yet at the same time I feel a strong attraction to the opposite sex. For maximum effect both the engine and the woman must be present. That's why our love making in the carousel engine room was so special. The paradox is as mysterious as the amusement park itself, which purports to bring joy but in fact exposes man's melancholy core.

"Just listen to those minor chords, the moan of the wooden trumpet, the storm wind howl of the strings. The organ knows how much we hurt inside. It cries for us. But, like me, it's trapped inside a wooden casing. No wonder it shouts so loud to be released from our bondage.

"And what do we do? We ignore it, let it fall into disrepair until one day it wheezes its last and gets pitched over the side of the pier or consumed in flames.

"Like the organ, I've been neglected and cry for the attention of a beautiful woman to rescue me, one who

understands engines and can patch my mechanical heart.
That woman is you. No one else will do. Don't you see?"

By the time I'd finished, Witte's scowl had smoothed to
a glaze of despair. Her eyes were raised to the rafters in
search of divine guidance.

"Like I said, you want your mother back." She sighed
forcefully in disgust. "I can't replace her, Karcher. No one
can. Long as you see her in me, I'll never please you. We
got no marriage with Nettie between us." The furrows
returned to her forehead as she drew a bead on my third
eye. "Now, either you cut the cord or you get along without
me."

Like a knife made of ice, Witte's insight cut me clean
and deep then quickly melted into reason, leaving no trace
of animosity. I was disarmed by the truth before I could
work up a defense, and the strange thing was, I didn't feel
condemned or helpless. I felt in control, a man and proud
to be one. Virulent in fact. So much so that I surprised us
both by scooping Witte up in my arms and bearing her off
at a brisk march (appropriately accompanied by Sousa's
"The Charlatan," boomed overhead by the Wurlitzer)
through the piling grove toward a maintenance shed at the
base of the pier.

"I'll show you who I think you are," I roared over the
sibilant surf between trombone blasts. The woman in my
arms squealed and struggled, but I could see again that tiny
void between her incisors.

"K-A-R-C-H-ERRRR," she growled, sounding the R,
"put me down."

"Not until you promise not to run away."

Keeping a firm grip on my squirming charge I kicked at the shed door. Fortunately the padlock wasn't fast. I picked it from the hasp with my pinky, hooked my toe under the door and tugged. As I turned with the opening door, Witte's long oval face emerged from the moon's shadow. Her huge gray eyes were following mine.

"Are you kidnappin' me?" she inquired in a pedal pitched whisper.

"I'm going to lock you in this shed until you agree to remain my wife," I said, stuffing her inside. She giggled.

Before my eyes could adjust to the dark, I stumbled over an empty five-gallon oil can. The gonging inside the tiny building was horrendous, and I was sure we'd be discovered. But all we heard during the long seconds we held our breath was snickering from the lovers we passed on the way to our hideaway and the putter of the Wurlitzer's rods between tunes.

Judging by smell alone, we could have crawled into a launch locker, so pungent was the odor of salted spruce, kerosene and oil paint. But the decor was right out of Nettie's workshop on the island.

A stout bench ran the length of the east wall. It was strewn with rusty wrenches and an open tin of Cabot's Cleaner in which a pair of oval, Namel-Var brushes were soaking, bristles on bottom and permanently set. Shelves above the bench held partly consumed and dribbling cans of enamel, mostly Wetherall's Truck and Tractor Green and Kirby's Black. Underneath were boxes of steel wool, rags and fasteners, just like Nettie kept them. Only the other three walls were wrong: no Stevens pump 22 on nails above the window; no weathered cedar board tacked with red squirrel tails over the door; no two-man cord wood saws hanging from spikes on the west wall; no Myers pump leathers wired together, dangling above the spare pump body in the corner. In their place hung the tools for ride maintenance: an assortment of huge wrenches, grease guns, hoops of steel cable and gasket sets for the donkey engines. Even the dimensions of the shed were the same as the one at Loonwater: eight by eight. And the door had the identical interior Z bracing and opened out to the right.

I began to feel queasy, put Witte down and sank to a nail keg. "Whew," I said, trying not to reveal my discomfort. "Guess we didn't disturb anyone important."

"'cept you. What's the matter now?"

"N...nothing's the matter. Why?"

"You look like Casper the friendly ghost."

"It's the moonlight, Witte. Makes everything look washed out." I breathed deeply but slowly and through my nose so she wouldn't notice.

Either I was getting better at hiding my feelings or Witte had decided to ignore them, for she settled into my lap and draped an arm around my neck. "Now, where were we, dear?"

"Arguing between the sixth and seventh piling."

I received a knowing and intolerant glance that quickly faded to a sexy smirk.

"Well, you're feeling better," she said, squirming provocatively and grinding her buttocks to emphasize her intentions.

My response didn't go unnoticed. "You drive an awful hard bargain, Buster."

The tape loop inside my brain had switched off under orders from my body which could no longer ignore Witte's advances. All I could smell now was wood smoke and lavender. The sea soaked spruce, the kerosene, the paint: all gone. The shed became simply a conveniently available shelter. I could have been anywhere, in public even. It didn't matter. All I could sense was the essence of Witte.

The organ had shut down, which meant it was past midnight, but I was so engrossed that I didn't miss its dependable throb or remember to check my watch until we staggered from the shack at moonset. Our consummation had consumed almost five hours, and the wonder of it was, I had no awareness of its duration nor any recollection of striking unpleasant props during the proceedings. I felt like I'd swum several slow miles in a heated pool: limp and buckling at the knees but without any points of pain. Evenly exhausted and unbelievably calm.

Witte on my arm was more severely debilitated than I. She gestured weakly in the direction of a rusty beach cart leaning against the south wall of the shed. "Fetch the barrow, dear." Her forehead furrowed with the effort of speech. "If we scrunch we can fit. Save a trip."

"Who's going to push us?" I asked.

"God, who got us into this," she slurred, smiling feebly up at me, her lips twisted with the wine of love.

I shall never forget the torment in her expression, more frown than smile. It didn't come easily to a principled woman battling better judgment with a face as long as

Witte's. The strain of indecision showed in every line barely bent by Cupid's bow. But she wanted to let me know it was good, good enough to gamble on our future together.

We tacked unsteadily through the pilings and out along the deserted beach. The "grunion" had returned to the sea, their tracks erased by the tide. In the east the sky was beginning to glow a sulfurous silver.

"Looks like a nice day," I offered optimistically.

"Got any aspirin, dear?" said a small voice from far below. Witte had sagged to a fraction of her five and a half feet and was almost entirely tucked under my arm. When she sneezed I felt the full impact of her jolt through my rib cage and winced for having kept her out so long in the raw. She swept the hair from her upturned face and mopped the spray with the back of her sleeve. "Huh?"

I dug in my opposing pants pocket knowing full well I had none. "We'll be home soon," was the best I could come up with.

Home. But which one? A spike of terror shot through my heart but this time I concealed it.

"I'll make you a nice pot of tea and snug you under the down comforter."

"Aspirin and steam, dear. Lots of steam."

Chapter 18

ON TRIAL

In the early morning light the still gently lit windows of the Murch farmhouse looked as peaked as Witte. I braked the Ford gingerly to a halt close to the kitchen door and helped her out. Tender new shoots of grass where Loring had seeded tickled our bare ankles with dew as we struggled to the stoop.

"Don't bother with me," Witte said, straightening after mounting the granite block. "You've only couple hours sleep before work. I'll be okay." She sneezed again and worked her key in the lock.

"I wouldn't dream of leaving you in this condition. Besides, I'd planned on calling in sick anyway."

As I let myself in behind her, Witte called over her shoulder on the way to the medicine cabinet. "You've got no excuse. I do."

I glanced at the Regulator: four fifty-five. "Shhhh... you'll wake your folks."

Ignoring me, Witte slammed the cabinet door, gulped three aspirin, pumped the Myers twice to its stop, stuck her mouth under the spout and slurped loudly. Then she attacked the Atlantic range. She spun open the draft, shook it down, dragged a lid aside and dropped in several splits of birch. Back to the Myers. Ten strokes to fill the kettle, which went on the front burner. The rending, rumbling and ringing sounded volcanic in the dawn stealth of the Murch kitchen, and it produced the expected results.

"What in blazes bit you, woman?" bellowed Loring, rubbing his eyes in the pantry doorway.

Witte replied without looking up. "Got a goddamn cold. You should have been up anyway."

"You, young lady, ain't even been to bed."

"More'n I care to," Witte muttered, avoiding my eyes.

"I see," said Loring, solemnly.

Witte seldom caught cold, but when she did, it set off a primordial ritual that began as soon as she reached the stove. Several times a day she'd stand on a chair next to the front burner, hang her head over the kettle and arrange her hair to form a tent about her face to trap the steam. There she'd stoop and steep until she felt herself start to reel, whereupon she'd step down, dash for the sink and plunge her face in a basin of cold water. She'd come up blowing spray and honking like a snow goose surfacing, bury her face in a towel then slather it with Noxema. I think the exorcism worked as well as it did because the germs had less shock tolerance than Witte.

The devil's mask, glazed, flushed and reeking of camphor, scowling at me across the table at breakfast that morning was a grim reminder of deeds overdone. I ate quickly and excused myself to check on Pattin who, miraculously, was still asleep in the guest room. While I changed her I overheard Loring sputter intermittently about priorities between mouthfuls of oatmeal.

Ida withheld comment until the dishes were cleared. She cornered us at the sink. "You can't catch up all in one night."

"Hadn't planned on it," Witte mumbled into the suds, her hands flying between the wash and rinse basins.

"No, guess you hadn't." Ida was eying me suspiciously. "Too nippy for parkin' without a heater this time of year."

"We weren't parkin'," Witte announced firmly without looking up or losing rhythm.

"Grassin' out in the williwags, then, I suppose?" Ida persisted.

"The Beach, Mumma."

"Lord, Witte. Lucky if you get off with just a cold."

"We weren't outside." Witte stifled a sneeze.

"Did it in a ride, did you?" Ida peered over the top of her glasses and winked at me.

Witte pulled her hands from the suds and without taking time to dry them placed them on her hips. She stood still for a second, hissing, then spun to face her mother. Her eyes were blazing like fire opals and she was shaking. "You're nose is long enough. Give it a rest."

"Well, I never..." Ida looked at me for support. Receiving none, she shrugged and started for the pantry.

"May I see you in the guest room for a moment?" I said to Witte who kept both barrels trained on her receding mother. She drew a deep breath then another. I saw her right foot start to rise and moved back instinctively. She stomped the floor once so hard the dishes rattled in the pantry, but Ida wisely kept silent and out of sight. Fortunately Loring was in the barn, too far away to hear the report. I reached for Witte's hand. Her eyes flicked focus in my direction. She sneezed again loudly. "Please," I said.

"Damn. She thinks I'm still sixteen." Witte blew her nose into a paper towel then followed me into the back room. I closed the door behind us. Pattin was in her playpen babbling incoherent instructions to Ida's rag doll, Damaris.

I opened in a subdued yet firm tone. "Witte, we have to talk. I need assurance that you'll..."

"Care for the both of you?"

I drew an index finger to my lips and continued quietly, fighting to suppress the quaver in my voice. "That's not fair. I'm just asking you for a commitment. We have a child to raise. Together. She needs a stable home. With *both* parents."

"Stable? With you? No, I hardly think so."

"Okay, a bit rocky. Sure. What marriage isn't?"

"More like stepping in marshmallow fluff."

I took hold of her shoulders. I wanted to shake the living hell out of her but forced my hands to relax their grip and remain still. "I love you, goddamn it. And I think you still love me, judging from last night's performance. Can't we give it another try?"

I felt Witte start to melt under my fingers, but she quickly stiffened and tossed her head back to draw a bead on my eyes.

"I'll give it a month. See how you make it through your birthday."

"You won't regret it," I said, trying to return her stare, but I had to close my eyes to block the tears. Slowly I drew her to me. She didn't resist. When her chest made contact I began to swoon, but her firm belly nudged me to my senses. Then her pelvis brushed my groin, tipped forward and settled there, forcing her thighs against mine. I felt my knees buckle. We started to topple. Witte, who was in better control, steered our fall so it ended on the bed which was thankfully nearby. I remember Pattin's little whoop just before we hit the mattress and her inconsolable bawling afterward. It seemed so congruent with the fragrant fever warmth of her mother's body.

After enduring my desperate embrace for more than a minute, Witte extricated herself and took pity on Pattin. Lifting her into her arms, she sang softly as she carried her to the bed and placed her between us.

> *Hush my darling, don't you cry.*
> *Mommy and Daddy will never lie.*
> *If you want to grow up strong,*
> *Repeat the words to this ole song:*
> *'Life is never easy, dear.*
> *Makes you sore and makes you tear.*
> *Tries your patience, burns your ear,*
> *But always whispers, love is near.'*

Pattin's howling subsided before Witte got to the refrain. By song's end her miniature Murch frown had dissolved. She lay motionless with her dark eyes fixed in wonder on the woman who timed our hearts. Then she fell asleep.

Witte carefully slid her arm from under Pattin and rose to her feet. "You better call Dory, dear. It's nearly seven. I'm going to tub up." She grabbed her white terry robe from the peg on the door and slipped out into the kitchen. I lay back beside Pattin and listened to the comforting stove noises in the next room and to the steady padding of Witte's bare feet on the back stairs. The rhythmic creak and clink of the Myers in the upstairs bathroom was all the lullaby I needed, and I soon joined my tiny daughter in slumber land.

* * * * * * * *

I awoke to the soft stroke of lavender scented fingers on my forehead. Witte was bent over me, looking down with the same tender expression she usually reserved for Pattin. With her head lowered, the skin about her face and neck sagged a little, suggesting a double chin and jowls which lent authority to her compassionate visage. Her eyes were no longer accusing but loosely focused deep among the silent shadows of the root cellar below us. Her hair was wrapped in a matching white towel and piled high, revealing her dainty, loving cup ears.

"You call in, dear?"

"I don't know how to use your phone," I said, sleepily. The Murch's still had a crank telephone on a party line as Varney was one of the last towns in southern Maine to switch over to the dial system. Loring had affixed its dovetailed oak box to the kitchen wall above the pantry port at a height convenient for him, which forced Ida to shout at the ceiling when she answered it. The bell generator's winding handle jutted from the right side. On the left the receiver dangled from its fork. Protruding from the front of the box was the adjustable mouthpiece which Ida kept lowered to its stop.

Witte straightened, drew her lips to a line and shook her head. She headed for the kitchen, leaving the door open behind her. From the bed I heard the receiver lift and the generator's unsteady whir.

"That you, Hilda? This is Witte. Get me Portland Copper, please." She paused briefly. "Yuh, he's bit under the weather. Been up most of the night. Yuh. Thanks, I'll tell him." After a long pause, "Dorrance Dillman, please. Stickney callin'." Another long pause. "Hello, Dory Dear. Witte, here." She sniffed loudly into the horn. "Look, Karcher's awful sick. Been up all night. Laid right out, poor thing. Yuh. Yuh. Tomorrow, I guess." She sneezed. "Thanks. I will, yes. You, too. Bye."

Mostly true I thought. Clever girl. I couldn't have been as convincing.

"Mumma's going to mind Pattin so we can get some rest," Witte explained, reentering the room with her mother close behind. I hadn't heard them negotiating the arrangement, but one look at Ida told me she'd been given little choice in the matter. Ida kept her eyes diverted as she reached for our sleeping cutie and made a hasty exit.

"Now we can have some privacy," Witte announced, locking the door. She glided to my side of the bed, opened her robe and let it fall to the floor. Tired as I was, the sight of her body back-lighted by the morning sun made me ache.

"God, you're beautiful," I exclaimed. "What man in his right mind wouldn't fight to keep you?"

"You're supposed to be asleep," she teased, crawling under the comforter and molding herself to me. "And you're still in your clothes, you naughty boy." She slid away and began to undress me. Too tired to protest, I rolled on my back and let her finish the job, boosting my hips twice to ease my dispanting. When she finished stripping me, she pulled the towel from her head and let her hair spill damp and limp across my chest. "Now, close your eyes."

I pretended to obey, but when I felt her hair dragging down my belly I had to peek. She'd about reached her target when she sneezed. That started her giggling, and she became so giddy that she collapsed on my thighs face down in my puckerbrush.

"Guess that'll teach me to seduce with a full head," she said, sitting up and blowing her nose in the sheet. She rocked forward, placed her palms on my chest and slid them up to my shoulders and off onto the pillow until she could no longer support herself. We came together mauling one another, rolling about and growling like a pair of lion cubs.

Despite her cold and our fatigue, Witte was determined to drain me once more before we slept. "Now, don't 'cha move a hair," she commanded, pulling away and sitting with her back to me on the edge of the bed. I studied her incredible silhouette while she swiped some ruby gloss on her lips and shaded her eyes with mascara.

It wasn't often that Witte adorned her facial features; they didn't need accenting. But when she was under the weather and needed to present a vigorous appearance she'd sparingly apply a little color. It was one of her rare little deceits.

When she finished she turned back, holding a Kleenex to her nose to suppress a sneeze.

"I'm in good shape," she said, shaking her head. But the locomotive eyes peering over the tissue revealed anything but distress; they were trained on a wet spot crowning a rise in the middle of the sheet. If there was any doubt about Witte's intentions, her pout, blotted in what remained of the tissue, left an unmistakably concupiscent impression.

"You sure are," I said, noting how her hair draped her left breast, barely able to conceal its nipple. "God would be hard pressed to build architectural curves more radically serpentine."

"Comes to architecture, dear, I'd say it's you that's hard pressed." With one graceful sweep she drew back the sheet, swung a leg over my head and pounced on my predicament.

Witte's body swaying above me, and what she was doing to me, so saturated my senses that I was forced to conjure a mechanical metaphor to maintain sanity:

It was a scorching July day. I was lying on my back, floating on an air mattress and drifting slowly downriver under a swing bridge. I reached up for the slender girder that stretched less than a foot above my chest and thrilled at discovering that my hands were nearly able to encircle it. I stretched to let my fingers trace the silky cables that suspended the span from substantial but resilient pylons poised high over my head. An engine started in the shed at the base of the pylons and oil began to drip onto my nose and lips and chin. As the bridge started to open, the rumble of the Reeves engine rotating the span paced my heartbeat's thunder. Drawn to the dark and din of the engine room, I pulled myself aloft to steep in the sweltering seat of power that churned there just for me.

Feeling a suction below, my brain began to reel and lost its lock on the metaphor. So instead of sinuous skeins of steel, my sated mind recorded only tender fronds of lavender. And the oil that flowed so freely, warm and clear and fatally fragrant was hardly the dingy crankcase dribblings from the Reeves. Instead of thinning under stress, its viscosity increased until it spun catenaries of ambrosia between my lips.

Again I fought to re-establish the mechanical metaphor to restore control. With clenched teeth I pulled down on the swaying girder and pressed my chin hard against the Reeves throttle. The engine raced. I felt the bridge shudder and hung on tight. A split second later, when the span reached its stop, the pylons took a seismic shock and quaked to their foundations. The vacuum abated, and above the roar of the Reeves rose a groan from the bridge horn so bovinely intimate, it couldn't possibly have emanated from a structure of cold steel.

Now weak and delirious from the heat of the machinery, I lost my grip, toppled from the parapet and plummeted to the river below.

How well I remember my fall. It was as protracted as it was inexorable, a timeless plunge into ecstasy. Witte later informed me that I'd nearly drowned the both of us. Fortunately we surfaced in a calm pool downstream, spent and gasping, wrapped in each other's arms and feeling decades younger, securely supported by a life raft in the shape of a bed. Sleep overcame our sated bodies before the secretions of seduction had a chance to dry.

* * * * * * * *

I awoke at sunset bathed in rose light and the glue of love. Witte was gone but her scent lingered on the bedding beside me. I buried my face in her pillow and inhaled deeply until my olfactory circuits were saturated with her bouquet. Outside my door I could hear the comforting scrape and scuttle of supper in the making.

A few moments later the door opened and in waltzed Witte wearing a white cotton jacket with shirred shoulders and double-flounced peplum dot-printed and piped in navy, a straight navy skirt, slit for walking and white pumps. Her hair was drawn back and clasped in a matching white barrette. She was holding a lavender lupine spike wrapped in a moistened wash cloth, but all I could smell was her Chanel Russia Leather.

"First of the year," she said, laying her leguminous offering on the pillow and settling on the bed next to me. "Gotta work tonight, dear. Supper's most ready. You must be starved."

"Mmmm, " I said, reaching for the top button of her jacket, but she drew her exquisite hand there to block my approach.

"Haven't you had enough?" She handed me the wash cloth and coyly twisted out of my grasp. "Better mop that puss before Ida sees you. Awful crusty." Rising, she thrust her chest defiantly in my direction before exiting.

"That's okay," I called after her. "I've already had supper." Getting no response, I washed my face then pulled on my rumpled, day-old clothes and smugly sauntered into the kitchen. Ida at the stove was the first to catch my eye.

"Sleep good, Karcher? Your color come up."

"Yes, thank you." Witte shot me a wicked grin from behind her mother's back.

"Guess you'll be wantin' to get back to town right after supper. Baby's things is all packed." She paused to slide the pot she was stirring to a cooler part of the stove. "Pork and beans all right, Karcher? They're my own; not Burnham and Morrill's, dear."

"Ida, to be honest, I'm so hungry, anything you cook is all right with me."

"You said you'd already had supper," Witte whispered close to my ear on a coquettish pass by.

Just then Loring appeared in the pantry doorway. "Well, you two seem to be hittin' it off good. Nothing like a workday rest to spruce up a marriage."

"I'm giving it a month," Witte confirmed from the stove, her face showing about as much expression as an almond slice.

"Hard woman," Loring observed, looking sympathetically in my direction before taking his place at the kitchen table.

The wood range no longer seemed adequate to chase my chill. I sat next to Witte with my back to the firebox and stared down at my plate. Save for Pattin's oblivious burble, we ate in disquieting silence for fear of fracturing the "thin ice" beneath the table.

Although certainly far from stable emotionally, I never got used to Witte's abrupt mood changes which, on the surface, resembled Nettie's. When Witte suddenly became dour, I'd instinctively flinch and cower, expecting next to see Nettie's hand or belt raised in retribution. Especially at times like this, when the course of my existence seemed to slat without direction, I had to remind myself that Witte, unlike Nettie, had a ground floor of engine-like consistency on which I could stand.

And yet, frightened as I was by Witte's volatility, I found her mood swings strangely congruent, almost seductive. After all, I grew up in a seesaw emotional atmosphere. I expected those around me to act mercurial. When they didn't, I became even more uncomfortable than when they did. For me it just wasn't home without conflict.

I somehow managed to signal this double message to Witte in a language that she could understand, and she, being optimistic, chose to view it favorably as a sign of my self-reliance, an essential ingredient to our continuing co-attraction. For if I had fallen apart when she became sullen or irascible, the game of love would surely have ended for us.

"I guess I'm on trial," I ventured finally, the beans gone from my plate. Ida rearranged the chips of ice I'd broken under the table with her feet, making a scuffling sound. Loring chortled, put down his fork and addressed Witte and me, looking sternly first at her and then at me. His tone surprised everyone.

"This house is not a courtroom, and I'm not a judge. Take your trial outside." He rose and pointed to the kitchen door. The rest of us scrambled to our feet in unison, producing a roar of chair legs scraping the unfinished pine floor. Witte plucked Pattin from the high chair and I grabbed the bags. We pecked Ida on the cheek and fled before Loring had a chance to redeem himself.

The last scene I recorded of our reunion at the Murch farm was that of a still startled Ida poised over the table full of dirty dishes and Loring's hulking frame stumping for the woodshed, his head rocking slowly from side to side.

"Yes, you are," Witte confirmed once we were sealed inside the Ford. I tromped the starter without answering her and backed the flivver away from the house. Through the windshield the weathered two-story Adam with its close-coupled train of annexes terminated by the outsized, hip-roofed barn, stood stark against the gathering dusk, its windows, not yet warmed by Aladdin's lamp, reflecting the ice-gray of Witte's eyes.

* * * * * * * *

In my rush to escape the Murch farm, the realization that our family was together again didn't hit home until I turned the key in the apartment lock. However tenuous, the reunion was finally underway. In a burst of joy I lifted Witte and Pattin from the pavement, kicked the door open and bore them across the threshold, one in each arm. When I plopped them down in the hall, Pattin, who was experiencing understandable insecurity, began howling and buried herself in her mother's coat. I closed the door gingerly behind me. Witte was eyeballing me.

"Go easy, Karcher. Trust takes time." Her delivery was deep and calm and the color had returned to her eyes. I put on the light and crouched to comfort Pattin. Witte remained standing, guarding our offspring with her voluminous feathers, while her exquisite hands stroked and cradled the little girl's head. Again above us now I heard mother recite in bass bell tones, "Life is never easy, dear. Makes you sore and makes you tear. Tries your patience, burns your ear. But always whispers: love is near." This time she was singing to both of us.

* * * * * * * *

The early days of June passed uneventfully. While I was at work Witte busied herself reverting the apartment from bachelor pad to home. I kept a low profile and assisted with the heavier rearranging only when my help was requested. The Saturday before my birthday Witte announced that Pattin needed a room of her own. "Her eyes and ears are getting too big for our bedroom. We'll wall off this end of the sitting room and build in an over and under bunk."

"Aren't you rushing the reunion a bit?" I chided. "My birthday's still a few days off."

Ignoring my quip she continued, "If you hurry you can pick up some studs at Chute's before they close."

She had it all planned: where the door would go and which way it would open; how we'd move the armoire from her bedroom at the farm and where it would fit; the design of the rosebud wallpaper and the color of the drapes she'd make for the window.

As I drove to the mill it occurred to me that my reinstatement had been established for some time. Although there had been no discussion on the subject, Witte had apparently decided to keep me, even to the point of expecting me to sire another child. Her plot both angered and thrilled me, and I vowed to discuss the matter with her as soon as I returned.

But in the ensuing bustle of building there were no convenient openings. I decided to keep my mouth shut and be grateful for any crumb of acceptance Witte bestowed upon me. It was not until the following Friday evening that I began to trust my role as husband and father.

We were grocery shopping at Shaw's. In the last aisle the idle market cart mysteriously began to jiggle and chug while waiting for Witte to decide on the appropriate vegetable to go with the chicken breasts she'd selected. She heard my stifled chuffing and put down the bunch of broccoli she was inspecting.

"Last time you did that, it was another woman."

Though her words were clipped, her simper told me that this time she knew it was for her. She returned to the vegetable counter, grabbed a solitary zucchini and placed it in the still gently rocking basket.

"What are you going to do with *this*?" I asked, stalling the engine and picking up the slender squash.

Without losing concentration, Witte strode off in the direction of the bread rack and tossed her answer over her right shoulder. "I'm a married woman. I'm going to cook it."

www.ingramcontent.com/pod-product-compliance
Lightning Source LLC
Chambersburg PA
CBHW060538260626
47161CB00003B/958